I0785045

◆ NESSUMSAR FAMILY ◆
LEGEND OF THE CROW

• Nessumsar Family •

LEGEND OF THE CROW

DEBBIE IHLER RASMUSSEN

M.O.M.M.
PUBLISHING

Mysteries of My Mind

Nessumsar Family: Legend of the Crow
Copyright © 2021 by Debbie Ihler Rasmussen

All rights reserved, including the right to reproduce this
book or portions thereof in any form whatsoever.

All rights reserved. Except as permitted under the U.S. Copyright Act of 1976,
no part of this book may be reproduced, distributed, or transmitted in any form or by
any means, or stored in a database or retrieval system without the written permission
of the authors, except in the case of brief passages embodied in critical reviews and
articles where the title, author and ISBN accompany such review or article.

For information contact:
authordebbieihlerrasmussen@gmail.com
Website: authordebbieihlerrasmussen.com

Published by:
M.O.M.M. Publishing
"Mysteries of My Mind"

Edited by: Audra Wright
Cover Design: Dee Loupeti • www.deegraphicdesign.com
Interior Design: Francine Platt • Eden Graphics, Inc. • www.edengraphics.net

Hello Kitty
Creator – Yuko Shimizu; Produced by Sanrio

Teenage Mutant Ninja Turtles
Created by Kevin Eastman and Peter Laird; Owners Mirage Studios and ViacomCBS

Captain America
Creator – Joe Simon and Jack Kirby; Owner Marvel Comics

American Girl Doll
Creator – Pleasant Thiele Rowland

979-8-9851721-0-2   Paperback
979-8-9851721-1-9   ePub
Library of Congress Number: Pending

This book is a work of fiction. Names, characters, places, and incidents either
are products of the author's imagination or are used fictitiously. Any resemblance
to actual events or locales or persons, living or dead, is entirely coincidental.

First Edition
Manufactured in the United States of America
10 9 8 7 6 5 4 3 2 1

DEDICATED TO:

Mason, Hayden, Hudson, Seth, Bella, Krista, Kiryn, Noah, Skyler, Leif, Natalya, Makayla, Gavin, Aspen, Zeke, Axle, Arian

With Love…

You can be anything you want to be…

OTHER BOOKS
BY DEBBIE IHLER RASMUSSEN

THE MYSTIC TRILOGY:

Mystic Angel

Mystic Lake

Mystic Mansion

MYSTIC TRILOGY BACK STORIES:

Best Friends Don't Leave

A Life of My Own

SPECIAL THANKS TO:

Adam Munoa Illustration

*Adam is the incredible artist — and friend — who drew
the caricatures for the original books for my grandkids.
He is amazing!*

Dear Readers,

IN NORWAY IN THE 1800's, the Relhi Family faced a dilemma—the younger generation rebelled against passing on the family's unique superhuman powers to their children.

In an act of rebellion, Rannug, with the support of his father, left Norway to start over in America, escaping—or so he thought—his superhuman powers, and his responsibility to avert the curse from his future children.

But the Relhi ancestors are relentless, and eventually come to America to seek the posterity of Rannug and bestow the gifts on them.

It took five generations for this to happen, and in an act of pure sacrifice, Rannug is faced with living between worlds to protect his young progenitors, or to move on to the spirit world and leave them on their own.

His decision is based on two things—his love for his grandchildren, and the absolute dangers he knows they will soon be faced with.

I have had fun using my last name (Ihler) and my kids last name (Rasmussen), both spelled backwards for this series. My ancestors on the Ihler side come from Norway and my kids' ancestors on the Rasmussen side come from Denmark.

This started out as Christmas presents to my grandkids in 2014. I decided to develop the stories into a series that I expect will be approximately eight books.

Incorporating superhuman powers, (each of my grandchildren chose their own in 2014) mystery, adventure and the paranormal, these books are full of exciting twists and turns.

Thank you for reading them and I hope you enjoy the adventure!

Love, Debbie

Prologue

Each generation will reap
what the former generation has sown.

— CHINESE PROVERB

THE SUN was just peeking over the majestic Rocky Mountains when Dede quietly came upstairs. She had started waking up before dawn since she was in pre-school, and now at nine years old, she couldn't sleep much past 5am. It was Saturday. She knew no one else would be up.

Or so, she thought.

She heard voices on the back deck, so she hurried to the closed blinds and peeked through the slats.

She could see her dad's angry expression, but she couldn't see who he was talking to.

"My dad left Norway to get away from this stupid family curse thing!"

"It isn't a curse—it's a generational genetic gift, one that you are depriving your offspring of."

"I am not depriving them of anything! I am protecting them, just like my dad did."

"Your offspring are not protected."

Dede couldn't help but notice the sudden fearful expression on her father's face. "What is that supposed to mean?"

"You have a daughter…"

"I have two daughters!"

"You know which daughter I mean." The voice sounded indifferent.

Her dad was silent as a black shadow rose in front of him—
the blackness spread across the deck and loomed in front of the
window.

Dede jumped back and the blinds snapped shut.

With trepidation she crept closer to the window and gently
opened the slats with her thumb and finger.

Blackness.

After a few seconds, she leaned even closer and slowly twisted
the wand so she could see more clearly.

Earlier the sun was shining brightly, now, only blackness.

Then she saw it.

A black crow. The image filled the window and its' cold black
eyes seemed to pierce right through her.

Dede froze.

❦ 1 ❧

PURSUIT

*There are generations yet unborn, whose very lives will be shifted
and shaped by the moves you make and the actions you take.*

— ANDY ANDREWS

SHE COULD HEAR two sounds.

Her breathing. Her heartbeat.

The dampness of lush tropical plants soothed her aching body, and she crouched lower snuggling deeper into the soft dirt.

Maybe she could simply disappear.

From its view at least.

High above the trees it swooshed back and forth, ever searching for its victim.

Her. It was searching for her.

Dede pulled her legs to her chest, buried her face in her knees, and wept.

But it kept up its vigilant patrol.

Her mind raced back thirty years to the nine-year-old little girl who peered out the window from the den in her parents' home.

The image had pulled her out of her thoughts, but now Dede quickly glanced around the dense forest. It wasn't cold, but she was shivering. She stayed in her makeshift shelter for what seemed like hours, listening to the constant swooshing of the predator above the trees. Finally, she fell into fitful sleep.

Dede tried to wake up, but the familiar dream took over.

3

She was nineteen, riding in her dad's new car. She and her parents were chatting as she leaned her elbows on the back of their seats. The setting sun was blinding, and Dad pulled the shade down.

"This car corners like a race car." he said.

But as they rounded a curve it must have been sharper than Dad expected, and they careened into the krail that formed a marginal barricade from the steep embankment.

The screaming of screeching tires pierced the air as Dede was ejected through the window. She skidded several feet on the pavement screaming from pain as the flesh peeled from her body. She slammed into something solid, and for a few minutes she lay still, unable to focus or move.

The air was strangely quiet.

Suddenly she thought of her parents and the pain intensified when she forced herself to roll onto her stomach, searching for the car.

Then she heard it.

A swooshing sound, and the slow, rhythmic flapping of wings.

She saw it now, a huge crow flying directly at her. Using every inch of her strength, she rolled out of its path, and it darted away from her.

But it circled back around and came at her a second time.

Once again, she evaded its sharp menacing talons.

But this time, the crow changed directions and Dede watched in horror as it glided, then stopped, above her parents' car, that was hanging dangerously over the cliff.

The crow hovered for several seconds, but then almost ceremoniously, it turned and looked directly at Dede, its black eyes locked on hers.

It looked down at the teetering vehicle and then, shooting straight up into the sky, it was gone.

In the distance she could see small black dots. They seemed

to be coming toward her, but she couldn't tell what they were.

Losing consciousness, she tried to focus on the dots, there were hundreds of them swarming above the cliff.

Then, loud creaking as the car, and her parents', fell into darkness.

Dede listened as it crashed down the steep ravine.

Silence.

Dede gasped and sat up. It was dark now. She could no longer hear the crow, but she didn't move. It was a relentless hunter, and it had been pursuing her for twenty-two years. She decided to stay right where she was until morning—just to be sure.

She fell in and out of sleep until the sun came up, then she slowly stood, stretched her back, and started her retreat from the safety of the Tropical Rainforest.

She had been coming to Hawaii every year for ten years. Kauai was her happy place.

She trudged through the foliage, but it seemed to be taking her longer than it should to get back to the path and the parking lot.

When she finally reached the edge of the dense forest she stepped out. Her sigh was audible, but her relief short lived.

How did she get so turned around to end up on the canyon side? Terrified, she did not take another step; she was within inches of plunging more than three thousand feet to sure death.

"Dede."

The deafening sound seemed to come from everywhere.

She turned to run back into the protection of the trees, but it was too late.

Dede knew what this meant. There was no escaping now.

She turned around slowly, and as she did her grandfather's tale of the story from Norway screamed in her head.

"Family of Reihi you will stand."

Sixteen-year-old Rannug stood along with the rest of his siblings.

Rannug's father Elo stepped forward, "Sir, I request once again, that this pass my children…"

Eras, the huge Nordic Viking stepped forward as well and stood within inches of Elo's face—but Elo just as massive in size, looked him straight in the eye.

Eras's eyes narrowed. "It is not possible. This curse, as you choose to call it, has been in your family for generations, and it is expected that it will continue—YOU are expected to continue. You have avoided it for eighteen years! This is your heritage, Elo!" Boomed the old Viking.

Elo glared at the senior Viking, and he considered using his own powers against the old man, but he knew the consequences of challenging a senior with the gifts.

Eras glared at him, but then his face suddenly soft-ened, "What are your concerns? Why would you not want your family to have this blessing?"

"Blessing? Maybe in the old days but it is almost the 1900's. Our ancestors have been accused of being witches. Burning at the stake? Thrown into pits? Stoned? No, not my kids. Not to mention, in this modern world—we stick out—we do not fit in. I don't want that for my kids, or any of my posterity."

Eras sobered. "You must make yourselves fit in, Elo." He paused thoughtfully. "I am told that your son, Rannug is leaving Norway for America next year. Even more reason to receive the gifts now."

"He will be back." Elo spat with conviction.

Eras turned slowly eyeing Elo, "Will he?"

"Yes . . ." Elo's voice caught.

Eras' hand shot up stopping Elo and he boomed. "Enough Elo!—It is done."

The ceiling of chamber rumbled as it slowly opened, spilling blinding sunlight over the entire room.

Elo raised a hand to shield his eyes but even then, he only caught a glimpse.

It entered—swooping over the heads of Rannug and his siblings and then it was gone. Elo stared into the sky as the ceiling rolled to a close with a loud thud.

It was done—Elo's efforts to protect his children and future posterity had been thwarted.

Dede saw the scene play out in seconds as if she had been there herself.

But right now, she was thinking of two warnings her grandfather had given her.

'It has to be within a foot of you. Stay out of its shadow.'

But there was no place to go. The crow's massive wings spread and swallowed her in blackness.

Frantically she glanced around—and the crow moved in closer.

The smell of wet feathers permeated the air and Dede tried turning her head away, but it was useless—she had lost all sense of control. Somehow, her will had left her.

Dede dropped her gaze to the ground as the crow gave her the directive her grandfather and father had been dodging since 1871.

Against her will, but unable to resist, she committed to a promise she hoped she would never have to keep.

～ 2 ～

A Weird Shape to Be In

TWENTY YEARS LATER

"I CAN'T BELIEVE you're going home next week." Elder Norton pulled his backpack on and shook his shoulders as it fell into place.

Mack grinned, "Me neither. I can't believe two years have passed."

They both looked up as two SUVs pulled into the dirt parking lot at the trailhead. The doors opened, and six more missionaries emerged all dressed in hiking gear and carrying backpacks.

They were all missionaries for their church, where it was standard practice to call them by Elder followed by their last name. They all followed that rule on a regular day, but out here like this, they dropped the elder, and used last names.

Four more hikers climbed out of the truck that parked behind the SUV. These were investigators, people the missionaries worked with who may be interested in joining the church.

An old, white-haired man walked around the front of the vehicle.

"Who invited the old guy?"

The man stopped and locked eyes with Mack.

"Huh?" Oblivious, Norton turned to where Mack was looking but in that second, the old man was gone.

"Who?"

Mack furrowed his brow, "Nothing, I thought I saw an old guy over there." He motioned to the SUV.

Norton shrugged, "I don't see an old guy."

Mack sighed, "Yeah." Puzzled, he shook his head, "anyway, this is the last hike for now."

"Yeah, but there will be more since you're coming back up here to school." Norton waved as the others' approached.

"This hiking thing for P Day is a great idea, Mack," said Elder Rigby.

P Day, a faster way to say Preparation Day, is pretty much a day off proselyting for the elders. Besides laundry and grocery shopping, the elders often participated in some sort of recreation. For Mack, his companion Norton, and several other missionaries in their district, hiking was the recreation of choice.

"I thought so. I guess it isn't normal for it to be so warm in Logan in December. At least that's what the locals say."

Elder Homer looked around at the crimson, orange, and yellow leaves, "Considering winter in Ogden last year, I'd say we are having a long Indian summer."

"Indian summer?"

Homer shrugged, "I don't know. That's what my mom calls it."

They all laughed, but immediately stopped laughing when a huge black crow suddenly dived towards them, swooping so low it almost touched Mack's head.

"What the?" Mack ducked and covered his head with both hands—so did everyone else.

"What was that?" Norton slowly stood.

The crow turned upward and shot straight into the sky.

Bewildered, they all looked at each other.

"It was a crow, right?" asked Rigby.

"I don't know, but if it was, it's the biggest crow I've ever seen." Mack stared after the massive bird that had now become a black dot in the distance.

Norton laughed, "It almost nailed you!"

"Real funny." Mack was startled by his feelings. The bird had come close to hitting him and that had scared him, but the tingling that passed through his body he could not explain. It was as though he had been shocked or something. He wasn't sure.

He was sure, but he was not about to share that part of the experience with these guys. He had a bit of a reputation of being a little eccentric and he had no intention of confirming that six days before he left. Besides, two new guys were here today. Better just to leave it alone.

The group gathered, and Homer explained where they were going. He looked directly at Mack. "You, okay?"

Mack scrunched his face, "Yes, it was just a stupid bird." He stood still for a few seconds as Homer eyed him. "Okay, if, you're sure."

"I'm sure," said Mack flatly.

Homer gave a brief description of the hike they were about to take but explained they may want to take a different trail when they came to a fork. He had not taken that path before.

The air was crisp, and the sun had not yet risen above the trees, Mack stepped out in front of the group.

Last chill day. Wow these two years have flown by.

Two years of missionary work for The Church of Jesus Christ of Latter-Day Saints had seemed like forever to many of them, but to Mack it didn't seem like there had been enough time to accomplish all that he wanted to get done. He came on this two-year mission to hopefully make some decisions about his life. He loved the outdoors and there wasn't a better place to hike than Utah. which they did every P Day, weather permitting. Or not, they often went out in the snow. He had an opportunity to work full time on a ranch after his mission, but he also was considering a career in marketing. This trip was to sort through his options.

When he first came to Utah he was torn. For nine months he had struggled, but now, he knew. Now he was okay to go back home, go to school, start a career, all that stuff that adults are expected to do. He was, he felt, prepared to face life back in the world.

Up until fifteen minutes ago he was certain of those goals. Now, something was different. If he were asked to explain he would have no words to express what he was feeling. He thought of the days and weeks before he left California and came to Utah. There were a lot of mixed emotions at that time.

But this wasn't the same. He didn't feel confusion or apprehension. Exactly the opposite. He felt an energy he had never experienced. He had been working out every morning for 20 minutes, so while going through this spiritual transformation these last two years he had also transformed his body and for several months he had felt healthier and much stronger than before he left home.

But now it was more. He felt alive—no, not alive, that was not the right word. Exhilarated! That's what he felt. Like a surge of electricity had passed through him. Like every nerve ending in his body had a new sense of awareness. He really did feel like he could do anything!

"Did you hear that, Mack?"

Mack whirled around to face Norton. "What? Uh, sorry. What did you say?"

Norton pointed past Mack. "They want to take that trail."

Mack nodded, "Sure, okay, that trail." He continued walking.

"Geez did that crow take your brain?" Norton laughed.

Mack scowled. "No, that crow did not take my brain. I was just thinking."

"About what?"

Mack turned onto the trail as directed. The incline was immediate, and he leaned forward a bit taking long strides.

"About what I'm going to do when I get home."

"School? Has that changed in the last ten minutes?"

Mack laughed, "No. Not that, I just mean…" he stopped and turned to face his friend. "I don't know, Norton, I feel like I can conquer the world."

Norton rolled his eyes. "That's different for you?"

"What's that supposed to mean?"

"I mean you have always had the get out of my way I've got this attitude."

Mack's eyes narrowed but he didn't immediately respond. He turned and started back up the path. "Yeah, I guess I sort of have."

But now I know it. I can do anything.

The group continued climbing the steep trail. They crawled around boulders and pushed through some overgrowth.

"Are you sure this is the right trail?" someone called from behind Mack.

"You guys chose it. I didn't," called Mack.

"Just seems like it hasn't been hiked in a while," said the same voice who, when Mack turned to look, realized it belonged to Jesse—one of the new investigators. In his mid-thirties, Jesse had been working with another set of missionaries, so Mack didn't know him well.

"I would agree with that," said Mack.

"But it will still get us to the top," said Norton.

"True." Mack heard Jesse mumble. "Eventually."

Other than small talk here and there, the group hiked in silence for at least another hour. The trail was steep and with their backpacks weighing them down, the climb required all their energy to maneuver through rocks, protruding branches and loose dirt. More evidence that the trail had not seen any recent hikers.

But the scenery was beautiful. The quiet clean air and the woodsy smell had a certain calming effect on Mack. He had learned to love these Utah Mountains.

Mack pushed a large pine branch out of his way and held it for Norton, and he and the others did the same. Once past the huge tree the trail flattened out a bit and then opened to a clearing surrounded by trees.

Each of the fourteen hikers found a place to sit down and almost simultaneously pulled out their water bottles or took huge swigs from their camel packs. Thin rays of sunlight peered through the tall trees, but up here among the pines, the air was much cooler.

Mack plopped down on a boulder and took a drink from the plastic straw attached to his camel pack. It was then that he realized he had not taken a drink at all—that he had not needed any water. He rubbed his bulging arms and then thighs. The tingling was still there.

He looked around at the others. Though not exhausted, they all looked a little spent. It had not been an easy hike to this point, but Mack did not feel any of that. He felt like he could run ahead all the way to the peak without much effort.

Puzzled by his own thoughts, he suddenly became aware of Norton staring at him.

"What?"

"I don't know. You seem…weird…"

Rigby chimed in. "Weirder…"

Mack laughed. "I'm not weird."

"Well, not in the sense of truly weird," added Homer. "But—yeah just a bit."

"Want to explain that?" Mack pretended to be offended.

"Well, yeah. Not too many guys admit they can change the world but remain somewhat humble. You have actually been pretty successful at that."

Mack laughed. "I don't know about the world." But even as the words fell from his lips a surge of energy seemed to pass through him.

Norton was still staring at him. "See, right there, that look. It's different."

"Different than what?" Mack stood quickly and when he did his entire body lifted off the ground at least a foot but then he landed back on his feet.

He looked around. All eyes were on him.

Mack's eyes darted from one person to the next and the next and finally he turned to Norton.

"Okay, that was a little weird," mumbled Mack.

"How did you do that?" Homer's eyes were wide.

"I just stood up."

"But it was like you jumped but then floated back down," Jesse was now on his feet. "That was awesome!"

"Yeah, but I didn't do anything special. I just stood…"

"Dude you floated—you like suspended in the air." Homer laughed. "Do it again."

Missionaries were assigned a companion. Once assigned, they learned to work together depend on and trust each other. Right now, all Mack could think of doing was turning to Norton, but his look was as bewildered as the other hikers.

"Say something," said Mack.

"Like what?" Norton chuckled. "You really did float."

Mack slowly sat back down on the boulder. He said nothing, but soon realized everyone was waiting for him to do something.

"Well?" The word drawled from Norton's mouth.

"Well, what? I just…" Mack stood and again he lifted from the ground. Only this time much higher, maybe three feet, but then he again drifted back to the ground landing on his feet.

This time Mack was visibly startled. "I…I have no idea why this is happening."

"Maybe it's the altitude." One of the other's stood quickly obviously disappointed when nothing unusual happened to him.

"The altitude?" Norton turned to the guy and rolled his eyes. "You're kidding me, right?"

"Well, what do I know?" said the elder whose last name was Pierce. "I'm from Kentucky."

They all laughed at Pierce's comment but that did not stop all of them from turning again to Mack.

He lifted his hands with his palms facing the group. "Seriously you guys, I don't know what's happening."

The conversation stopped when they heard something coming through the trees. Whatever it was, it moved quietly.

"That can't be a person," whispered Homer.

"Why not?" asked Rigby.

"Because people make more noise than that."

"Unless they are sneaking up on someone," said Norton.

"Who would be sneaking around up here?" asked Mack.

Norton shrugged, "I don't know." He turned toward the sound which was directly behind him. "Hey who are you?"

Silence. The sound immediately stopped.

"What the?" Norton turned to Mack.

But then total chaos.

"Norton!"

"Look out!"

"Run!"

The commands were yelled or rather screamed, and Mack had no idea who said any of them. He saw Norton, but he didn't see what the rest of them did.

A huge cougar leaped from the trees. Its massive paws touched the ground at one point but then it was air born again heading straight for Norton.

Mack stood and as he did, he again felt his body lift off the ground. Instead of running, he leaped toward Norton. He raised one hand—suddenly feeling detached from his body, he saw the claw of a bear in front of him. He was looking down on the frightened Norton and the cat who had now pounced on his friend pinning him to the ground.

Mack took another step toward the cat and with one swipe of his hand he threw the huge animal off Norton. It landed on its back several feet away but immediately scrambled to its feet. The cat snarled and crouched ready to pounce again.

Without hesitation Mack ran toward the cat, but he found himself running on his hands and his feet. Though confused, he still charged the cat as instinct took over.

The cat did not move, and Mack did not stop. He stood again only this time he seemed much taller than before as he looked down on the cat.

The cougar leaped at Mack, and he felt the cat's claws sink into his shoulders. He pushed it away and swinging his arm across his body he smacked the cat on the side of the head again sending it sprawling across the ground.

Again, the cat found its footing, crouched, and faced Mack.

Finding himself on all fours again, Mack stood. He froze staring into the fierce green eyes of the crouching cougar, its eyes locked on Mack's.

For a few seconds Mack heard nothing. His chest heaved and not taking his eyes from the cat, he reached up to wipe the sweat dripping from his mouth, He found the motion awkward and dropped his hand to his side.

The cougar's top lip had been curled back bearing its sharp teeth but now it seemed to cower. Still crouched but backing away too, it did not avert its glaring eyes from Mack.

Suddenly spinning around, the cougar sprang from its position and with two leaps disappeared into the trees.

"Geez…" began Mack, but all he heard was a low growl.

He turned again reaching for his mouth. He glanced at his hand—which was not his hand at all. It was a claw—a huge bear claw.

Panic seized Mack and he turned to the group of hikers. He was looking *down* on all of them.

All were staring at him with wide frightened eyes. Some of them were peering at him from behind trees, a couple of them had taken cover behind boulders. Only Norton had not moved. He lay on his back staring up at his friend.

The fear in Norton's eyes made Mack cringe and for a second, he forgot his own fear. He reached for Norton's hand, but he did not respond.

Suddenly a sharp tingling passed through Mack. Still reaching for Norton's hand he saw the look on his companion's face turn from fear to bewilderment and Norton scrambled to his feet.

"Are you okay?" As he spoke, the words sounded funny inside Mack's head.

Norton said nothing, he just backed even further away.

"What's wrong? Did that cat hurt you?"

Finally, Norton spoke. "What's wrong with *me?* You're the one who's bleeding."

Mack looked down. He was not wearing a shirt and blood oozed from deep scratches on both of his shoulders. He looked behind him. His shirt, jacket, and pants were torn to shreds—scattered haphazardly on the ground. His shoes and socks appeared to have been thrown in all directions. His backpack lay untouched near the boulder he had been sitting on.

He was naked!

Mortified Mack spun around, ran to his clothes, and picked up what was left of his pants. He snatched his backpack, digging around until he pulled out a pair of sweats he had thrown in at the last minute.

He pulled the sweats on and turned quickly to face the other hikers.

No one said anything.

"What—what just happened?" Mack choked on the words.

Norton stared at him in disbelief. "Dude, you were like…you turned into a…you confronted that cougar…you…who *are* you?"

Mack stood silently. The tingling had almost gone away, and he now felt the pain in his shoulders. He felt tears welling up in his eyes. Embarrassed he tried to force them back.

Apparently seeing his vulnerability, the hikers slowly emerged from their hiding places and encircled Mack.

Norton pulled a first aid kit from his backpack and gently pushed Mack to a sitting position on the boulder. He dabbed at the scratches on Mack's shoulders. "Some of these may needs stitches."

Again, Mack choked. "I'm not going to a hospital."

"Looks like you won't need to." The voice was a whisper, and it came from Jesse.

Mack looked down at his shoulder. The scratches were almost gone, and the pain had nearly ceased as well.

A low whistle escaped through Norton's pursed lips.

"What happened?" Mack asked quietly.

"Well, you turned into a bear," said Homer nonchalantly.

Mack's eyes narrowed and he studied each of their faces. Everyone was nodding.

"A bear?"

"A very large bear," Norton nodded.

Mack dropped his head. "That's ridiculous, and unbelievable."

"Agreed," said Homer. "I would never believe this if I hadn't seen it with my own eyes."

"I don't think we should tell anyone," Mumbled Mack. Suddenly his thoughts raced. He thought of the crow and how he had felt since it had swooped so close to his head.

He looked at Norton. "You don't think that crow…?"

Norton nodded. "Man, I have no clue."

Again, there was silence.

Mack was at a loss for words.

But obviously Rigby wasn't. "Dude! That was awesome!"

Mack nodded.

What did happen? I must be crazy—or all of them are crazy. It's probably good that I'm going home.

Even so, he wasn't sure he wanted that to happen to him again.

But—it was awesome.

He looked around at the other hikers—their expressions spoke loudly. They were in awe—or bewildered—he wasn't sure, maybe both.

Mack now drank nearly all the water from his camel pack. The cold water cooled his throat and lungs. He stood—and when he felt he was lifting off the ground again, he quickly sat back down.

His hiking companions moved closer now, but amid their confusion and questions Mack could only see one thing, the old man he had seen earlier, behind the group of friends, only briefly, and then he was gone.

$\backsim$ 3 $\backsim$

VOICES

TAKING A NEEDED BREAK, Haydee jogged off the soccer field toward the bench. She was startled to see an old, white-haired man, standing nearby. She glanced around but when she turned back, he was gone. She shrugged and plopped on the bench between two equally exhausted teammates. She opened a bottle of water and drank half of it before saying anything.

"I hate playing this team. We can always be sure one of us is going down," she scoffed.

Carrie sat next to her and nodded in agreement. Careful not to point she motioned in the direction of two players on the opposing team. One a short stocky blonde and the other a redhead—a little taller than the blonde, but equally as stocky.

"Looks like they have been assigned the target today," said Carrie.

Haydee nodded. "It does seem that way. And they are after Sydnie."

Talya was sitting on the other side of Haydee and leaned toward her two teammates. "Maybe we need a strategy of our own."

As much as Haydee and Carrie agreed, they all knew their coach's philosophy and there was no way he would allow his team to win by using a plan to take an opposing team member out of the game. It happened a lot in college sports—everyone knew it—in fact, it was pretty much accepted.

But not to Coach Henderson. He had a lot of old school ideas about honor and winning and playing fair, stuff like that.

Most of the time Haydee agreed with him but when they played this team, she felt like throwing all honor out the window and simply kicking butt on some of these players. She sighed. Coach Henderson called Talya back into the game and Haydee yelled when she left the bench, "We got this!"

Talya shot her left thumb in the air as she dashed back onto the field.

Haydee knew she and Carrie would be back in the game soon and for a brief second, she leaned back, closed her eyes, and stretched her neck from side to side.

"Haydee look out!"

Haydee's eyes jerked open just in time to see a huge black crow flying directly at her. She fell backwards off the bench as the bird swooped within inches of her face cawing as it went. She rolled over and watched as the bird shot straight up and became a black dot in the distance.

"Are you okay?" Carrie extended her hand and Haydee welcomed the help to get to her feet.

What in the heck…?

Several teammates surrounded her, and Coach Henderson pushed his way through.

"Haydee are you okay? What happened?" the words tumbled from the coach's lips.

Haydee heard a whistle from the field, and she knew they had called a time out. She felt ridiculous with so much attention suddenly focused on her, and she quickly brushed the subject aside.

"It was just a bird. It didn't see it coming because I had my eyes closed."

Carrie rolled her eyes. "That stupid bird was heading right for you!"

"Maybe, maybe it didn't see me," sputtered Haydee. "Anyway—I'm fine, honest. It just scared me."

Coach Henderson studied her for a few seconds and then he patted her shoulder. "Okay then." He turned and walked back onto the field.

Seconds later the game resumed.

Haydee sat back on the bench. Her entire body tingled, and she wondered if she had injured a nerve or something when she hit the ground.

She stretched her arms and neck—no everything felt fine—but still the persistent tingling.

'Too bad she didn't break her neck.'

"Excuse me?" Haydee blurted.

"Huh?"

Carrie looked puzzled.

"Did you say something?" asked Haydee.

"No." Carrie gave her a confused side glance and then leaned over and went back to tying her shoelaces.

Haydee slowly nodded and she involuntarily found herself searching the sky for the crow. It was long gone.

Coach Henderson called Carrie back into the game, but this time Haydee said nothing. She felt confused as the incessant tingling continued to course through her body. She looked in the direction of the two girls she and Carrie had talked about earlier. They were on the other side of the field, and both had their backs to her.

Haydee sighed.

'We should get the one who nearly got smacked by that bird. She looks a little dazed.'

'I'm glad Coach already has her targeted for the game next week.'

'I hope we win this one.'

Haydee jumped up and clapped both hands to the sides of her head. *What is that?!*

Anxiously she looked around. No one around her was talking—at least not to each other. They were yelling from the sidelines encouraging their team.

"Haydee!"

She looked up. Coach Henderson was motioning for her to come back in the game.

Haydee nodded—looked around again and trotted toward her coach as she looked over at Carrie.

'*That was so weird. Oh, good she's coming back in.*'
Haydee stopped short.
"C'mon Haydee, hurry up!" Coach was now demanding.
'*What's wrong with that girl?*'
Haydee shook her head. *Nothing's wrong with me! Where are all these voices coming from?*
Trying desperately to concentrate she took her position on the field. The play started, and her team began moving the ball down the field.
'*Get in position.*'
'*I need to be over there.*'
"*Only five more minutes.*'
"Dribble!" The voices were confusing, but that last word came from Talya, and then she yelled, "What are you doing, Haydee!?"
"I'm…!" Haydee tried to focus on the ball at her feet and automatically began dribbling it down the field. A defender came directly at her and attacked the ball. Haydee lost her footing. The ball was now in possession of the opposing team.
She scrambled to gain possession back, but another of her teammates interceded and once again Haydee's team was in the attacking position.
Haydee knew exactly what would come next and she positioned herself for the expected pass. It came and Haydee knew a header was necessary, but as the ball approached again, she heard several different voices almost at the same time.
'*She never misses!*'
'*Miss!*'
'*Back her up!*'
'*Get the ball!*'
Haydee's head was spinning. She glanced away only for a second but enough time for the ball to smack her on the side of the head knocking her off balance. Fortunately for her, Talya was nearby and regained possession. However, a yellow card went up—Haydee had no idea why—and the game briefly stopped.
Coach Henderson took the opportunity to take Haydee out of

the game and she once again found herself sitting on the bench. Only this time, the team doctor, who had been accompanying the team for all the Pacific Coast Athletic Conference championship games, was fussing over her.

"Haydee let me look at your eyes?"

"Why?"

"I'm wondering if maybe you have a concussion."

"From what?"

"You fell off the bench, right?"

"I landed on my *back*."

"Oh…" the doctor held Haydee's face in his hands and looked directly into her eyes.

Haydee pulled away. "It's not that anyway—it's the voices…" she immediately noticed the startled expression on the doctor's face.

"Voices?"

"Or sounds or something…or…whatever…I just can't seem to concentrate."

The doctor checked her pulse, looked into her eyes again and shook his head. "What do you mean, voices?"

Haydee shrugged, "Nothing, I…I don't know. It's no big deal."

The doctor patted her knee when he stood. He walked away from her and directly toward Coach Henderson.

Great. What an idiot! Why did you mention voices?!

Haydee sat alone at the end of the bench. Melissa, a substitute player, sat a few feet away from her, but she was not looking in Haydee's direction.

'Maybe I'll get a chance to play this game.'

Haydee winced realizing her teammate was hoping to play now that Haydee was out of the game. She looked across the field at the stocky red-haired player she and Carrie had been talking about earlier.

'We've got them now —Shabam!'

Haydee turned to her coach who was talking to two of her teammates. He glanced in Haydee's direction.

'I guess she is down for the count this game.'

She leaned forward with her elbows on her knees and plopped her face in her hands. Suddenly she realized something. *If I look right at someone, I can hear what that person is thinking. But why? How come I can hear them at all?* It seemed that she could hear several voices—but at other times—like now—all the voices were quiet.

The tingling sensation had all but stopped. She could feel it only in her hands. She slowly sat upright and methodically looked from one person to another—testing her newfound phenomenon—she looked across the field now at the blonde opposing player who was approaching another player on her team.

'*We need to make a plan.*'

Haydee turned to the player the blonde girl was walking up to.

'*Oh, here she comes—she'll have some lamebrain idea of how to get rid of the player coach targeted for her and Cath.*'

"What the…?" Haydee jumped to her feet. Time was moving fast—the game was almost over, and the score was tied. She had been no help to her team in the second half, but she had to do something now.

The teams were taking their places on the field and the other team had possession.

How did that happen?

She immediately dismissed the thought knowing what she needed to do.

Sydnie was one of her team's best kickers' and second to Haydee in scoring. The redhead and the blonde were targeting Sydnie.

Since it was obvious to Haydee that Coach Henderson was not putting her back in the game, she now had to convince him to. She first needed to make sure she could control her newfound mind reading skill and she once again tested it by looking directly at one of her teammates.

'*I hope Matt is here.*'

Are you kidding me?! She is thinking of her boyfriend at a time like this?! Haydee rolled her eyes, "Wow."

She turned her attention to the two opposing players.

First the redhead. *'I'll be on her left side—must take her out before they get possession. She can't get the ball, or they will score. The only other way is if we score before they get the ball.'* The girl chuckled to herself. *'Shabam!'*

"What is that some stupid code word for kill?" Haydee looked at her own team lineup and laughed, "Fat chance." But she did know that they could take Sydnie out of this game, and if they were successful, would likely put her out of the next game as well.

Haydee watched as her team took their places and she noticed that the redhead was in position to guard Sydnie. The blonde and the redhead would most likely provide defensive pressure on Sydnie—if she got the ball—which Haydee knew was definite. The blonde was in the midfield anchor position. Because Haydee knew what their plan was, she also knew Syndie would not have a chance. It was classic cheating—but this team was highly skilled in their tactics.

Her own team was setup for a familiar play—and because it was almost always successful, Haydee also knew that Coach Henderson would use it. With all the tension, he may not even notice the two opposing team members who were now strategically placed to destroy one of his best players. The game was tied, and this all-important game would determine which team would go on to compete for first place next week.

Haydee looked at the blonde. *'When she goes down, I just need to trip and fall on her leg so that I can twist it or knee her in the chest. Either way should work.'*

Haydee cringed and she immediately turned and ran toward Coach Henderson.

"Coach?!"

"What, Haydee?" but he didn't look at her.

"Coach, listen."

"Haydee it can wait."

"No, it can't!"

His eyes narrowed, and he turned in her direction. She recognized that look. It was the 'how dare you bother me at a time like this' look. They *all* knew what that meant. But she was a team captain, so he might listen.

Haydee blurted, "just move Sydnie. Run the other play—put her on the opposite side and…and put me in."

"What? No Haydee, your head is not in the game today."

"Coach!"

He glared at her.

"I mean, Coach, please. Put me in where Sydnie is and move her to the other play position. We can still score! Trust me…*please.*"

Haydee was one of this team's best players and she knew Coach Henderson believed that. But he was not likely to take Haydee's advice at this crucial moment.

She grabbed his arm, which was completely uncharacteristic of Haydee.

Puzzled, Coach looked right at her. "What do you want, Haydee?"

"*Please*…please, move Sydnie and put me in her place."

"No can do."

"Coach you *have* to!"

This time everyone around them stared at Haydee.

"Have you lost your mind?" Coach snapped at her but then he stopped and briefly stared right into her eyes. He shook his head and Haydee heard what he thought. *'What am I doing?'*

"The right thing!" Haydee grinned and she ran onto the field.

"What the? How did you?" Coach Henderson yelled after her.

"Sydnie, your taking Nell's position—she's out for this play."

"What? Why?"

"Trust me—just go."

Sydnie looked over at coach who was motioning for her to move to the other position, but at the same time he was shaking his head.

He hates me right now.

Nell ran off the field as Sydnie took her place and Haydee fell into position smack between the blonde and the redhead. They both glared at her, and she just smiled.

Suddenly, between her and the two girls, the old man was there, briefly, but then he was gone. For a second Haydee froze.

'What does she think she's doing?' The redhead's thoughts were a snarl.

Haydee snapped back to the game, "Why, playing soccer—what are you doing?" Haydee touted her and the redhead's face suddenly contorted, and her hair seemed to light on fire.

The ball was in play now and the attacking team started the ball down the field only to be thwarted and Haydee's team took possession.

Talya dribbled the ball toward the corner and passed it to Carrie, who in turn was supposed to pass it to Sydnie—in the position Haydee was in now. Carrie looked confused for a second but then passed it to Haydee.

That was not supposed to happen—at least Haydee hadn't considered it happening, but she slowed the ball with a chest trap allowing her team mate to execute a skillful chip pass over their heads and directly at Sydnie.

A perfectly played break by three teammates put Sydnie in position for a breakaway and she took a perfect chip shot. The ball sailed above the goalie's head and dropped just under the crossbar and into the net.

"Score!" Haydee jumped in the air. When she did, she purposely chest bumped the opposing blonde knocking her to the ground.

The whistle blew, and the game was over.

Haydee looked at the bewildered blonde and redhead and extended her hand to the girl she had knocked down, but the girl shrugged and scrambled to her feet.

"Oh, by the way…"

The two girls glared at Haydee.

"I think that's what you two call a shabam!" she laughed and ran to join her celebrating teammates.

❦ 4 ❧

DANGEROUS RIVALRY

THE WHISTLE BLEW and both teams climbed out of the pool. Angry comments were flying from both sides as the coaches tried to get the players on both teams to line up for the traditional handshake at the end of every game.

But this was no ordinary game. The Nighthawks were in first place now, and the Sharks wasted no time in accusations of cheating.

Harley found his towel and began drying off as did some of the other players, but they were all distracted by more than just name calling. Harley turned to see Nate Simmons, the Nighthawks team captain approaching one of the Sharks.

There was an old man with white hair walking right behind Nate.

What the…?

The old man found Harley, and they locked eyes for a few seconds, and then he was gone.

Harley stared in the direction of the old man but was pulled back to the present when he heard Nate.

"Listen, you stupid jerk, the next time you hold me under the water like that…!"

"You'll what?" The tall senior from the losing team took two steps toward Nate.

He shoved Nate who fell backwards but immediately recovered

and dived at his attacker. Nate wrapped both arms around the other kid's waist and the two of them crashed to the pool deck.

This had been an intense game and an unexpected loss for the defending high school champions and none of their players were taking it well. Neither were their coaches.

Harley hung back. Tall, muscular, unassuming, and shy by nature, he had started water polo as a freshman and fought to earn his place on this team. But learning to be aggressive, even as a water polo player had been a challenge for him—and when it came to physical confrontations, such as were happening right now, he never wanted to get involved. What was the point? They had already won the game and in his opinion, they should just get back in their cars and go home the victors and leave the defeated team to wallow in their grief.

But only he and a couple of his teammates felt that way. The rest of them wasted no time in defending their 'honor'. Especially Nate, the hotheaded captain.

Harley knew that Nate had good reason to be mad. The other kid had held him under the water several times throughout the game, but Nate always emerged the victor so why couldn't that be good enough?

Because it wasn't. Not to Nate. He could never let things go and this time was no exception.

Harley watched as the ensuing battle began to unfold. It always started with Nate, but before long the co-captain and most of the other seniors would engage someone in an argument, and soon, nearly the entire team would be involved in the brawl.

Typically, the Nighthawk's coaches would step in and attempt to thwart the fights, usually gaining control after a few name callings and well-placed hits had already found their marks. But today was different, even the Nighthawk's normally mild-mannered coach had exchanged words with the other team's assistant coach after a bad call by the ref, so now the two of them were head-to-head in a heated argument.

Harley was not sure what to do and it appeared neither were Ren and Marc, two freshman teammates who stood with him on the bleachers. He found his parents in the crowd who were making their way in his direction. Other parents were scrambling down the bleachers as well, all heading toward the mass of brawling boys.

Fights were breaking out all around Harley, but he held his position.

Brad Cowan, one of the other senior Nighthawks was shoved into the bleachers where Harley stood. Brad crashed to the deck but jumped back to his feet and whirled on Harley, Ren, and Marc.

"What's with you guys?! Harley, you're one of the biggest kids on this team! Why don't you come down off the bleachers and help us?!"

Harley did not respond. He was struggling with that very concept. Why didn't he feel compelled to jump into the middle of the fight? But even as he struggled with the thought—and tried to reason his way to jump into action, he knew he wouldn't do it. Fighting had never made sense to him.

The scene was complete chaos. The two water polo teams clad only in speedo swimsuits—most of them having pulled off their caps before getting involved—were brawling either on the pool deck or in the water. The four coaches were involved in a yelling match on the opposite deck from where Harley stood, and even several of the parents representing both teams had joined the complete disorder.

A few parents from both teams were attempting to stop some fights and two mothers were calling to their kids from the side of the pool, but they weren't having any success in getting their boys to stop.

The entire pool area was in pandemonium and except for Harley, his two teammates, and a couple of guys from the opposing team, everyone seemed to be contributing to the confusion. It was right then that Harley heard Ren.

"Holy cow, look at that bird!" Ren ducked but both Harley and Marc stared in disbelief.

"What the?" Harley was not sure if he was seeing what he *was* seeing. "Is it a crow?"

"If it is, it's the biggest crow I've ever seen," and Ren crouched even lower.

The massive black bird seemed to be flying directly toward them. Mesmerized by its sheer size Harley watched as the bird approached, but as it got closer it seemed obvious that the bird had every intention of flying right into Harley.

Marc grabbed Harley's arm and pulled him down onto the bleachers just as the bird swooped narrowly missing Marc.

The bird shot straight up, but then turned abruptly and dove again, this time knocking off Harley's cap that was unsnapped and sitting loosely on his head.

The bird bolted sharply upward and disappeared into the clear California sky.

Harley struggled to regain his footing on the wet bleachers, all the time staring after the bird.

"Do you have a death wish or something?" Ren shook his head. "Why didn't you get out of the way?"

"Did you see the size of that thing?" said Harley.

"Yes, I did, and I was expecting it to take your head off the way it flew right at you."

Ren looked down, "Well it did take your cap off."

Harley nodded absently.

Why didn't I move? What compelled him to simply stare at the oncoming attacker? He was confused by his own inability to decide at that split second.

Suddenly, Harley felt as though he was in a fog. He could still hear his two friends debating the seemingly near-death experience Harley had just encountered, and he could still hear all the commotion caused by the ongoing fighting and yelling, but he seemed to be somehow removed from the scene—although he was still there. Everything sounded distorted and distant.

What had been complete and utter chaos a few seconds ago now seemed to move in slow motion. He looked across the water and noticed his parents concerned looks, but even they seemed to be moving slowly now. He turned to the mass of scantily clad tan bodies whose anger only seemed more intense, but every punch moved slowly through space, and when it hit its mark, the effect on the recipient was magnified for Harley in sight and sound.

Harley clamped both hands to his ears, but the loud grunts and groans continued to permeate his hearing adding to his confusion.

Suddenly, two angry players from the other team charged the bleachers and pulled Ren and Marc to the cement. One landed a well-placed hit on Marc's jaw and the other pushed Ren down onto the deck.

A third player came from behind Harley and pulled both of his arms behind him, locking them in a painful hold.

Harley winced, "What's the matter with you guys!?"

At the same instant Harley saw the big kid and Nate who were still fighting. The kid grabbed Nate by the neck and head butted him so hard, Nate fell into the pool. Harley watched in horror as Nate sank into the water making no attempt to get out.

He's unconscious!

Harley struggled with his attacker, but to no avail—now another had joined them and punched Harley in the gut.

He gasped and doubled over not taking his eyes off Nate.

"Get off me you idiots! Can't you see Nate is hurt? He's in the water!"

"It's his own fault! Let him drown!"

Harley was mortified. "You don't mean that! Let me go! Coach! Coach!" but the angry coach did not hear him.

Harley pulled his arms free and pushed his assailants away but was immediately seized and pulled into a choke hold by the guy who had hit Marc. Harley struggled to keep his eyes on Nate.

"Someone help him! Nate is drowning!" Harley yelled as loud as he could but still no one responded.

Harley found his parents and his eyes locked with his mothers. "Mom! He's going to die!"

At that second a surge of what felt like electricity coursed through Harley's body. His eyes narrowed as he anxiously turned again toward the pool. Pulling both arms to his sides, he threw his self-appointed opponent off his back. *He has to get out of the water!* And suddenly—like watching a movie—Nate was lying on dry concrete at the bottom of the pool.

Immediately, Harley saw something that startled him. The water seemed to be moving, no, parting. Harley turned his gaze away for a second and when he did, the water settled back. The thought suddenly occurred to him that somehow, he was controlling the water.

Unconsciously, he grabbed his swim cap and pulled it on—when he did, everything around him became sharp and clear. The colors, the sounds, everything.

But how?

Right now, it didn't matter how. Nate needed help and only Harley seemed to notice.

Harley concentrated his gaze on Nate and again this time he said out loud, "He has to get out of the water!"

Again, the water immediately began receding and in seconds Nate was lying on the dry pool bottom.

All commotion stopped as everyone's attention turned to the pool. A hush fell over the crowd.

Two of Nate's closest friends spotted Nate and jumped into the empty end of the pool.

Someone must have called the police, because three officers and two paramedics ran into the crowd. The paramedics jumped into the pool alongside the two teammates and all four coaches who were now surrounding Nate.

The paramedics lifted Nate onto a stretcher and then out of the pool and placed him on the deck. As they emerged, the water rushed back, sweeping the unsuspecting swimmers and coaches into its current before settling and gently lapping at the deck.

Empowered now, Harley turned to the three startled boys who had attacked him, Marc, and Ren, and shoved them away from him.

Something had happened. He was not sure what, but he felt a strength he had never experienced, and for some reason he was able to control—things!

He looked at the three baffled boys who were backing steadily away from him.

He glanced around locating several game balls lying in random places around the pool. He visualized the balls hitting those three boys and immediately the balls flew from their resting places and began pelting the three now terrified players.

Harley laughed as the boys ran from the bleachers, but to no avail as the balls followed them hitting their bare backs, bouncing off and hitting again.

Finally, Harley turned away and the balls each fell to the pool deck and slowly rolled haphazardly until they stopped.

Harley turned to the water again and imagined it drenching the two water polo teams. In seconds, the water began churning and a whirlpool formed in the center. The motion threw water onto the two startled teams, forcing them away from Nate, his parents, and the paramedics.

He wanted to see if Nate was okay, but Harley knew if he turned his head the whirlpool would stop. Finally, he did, and the teams scrambled away from the pool deck.

He was relieved to see Nate raise his hand and rest it on his forehead as he was moved onto a gurney.

Harley ran towards Nate, whose eyes were open, and he glanced in Harley's direction. Before Harley could reach him, Nate was whisked away followed by his parents and their Coach.

The crowd was dissipating now amid startled comments about the water, Nate, and the kids getting hit with water polo balls.

Harley chuckled.

He sighed, suddenly becoming aware of someone behind him. Turning around slowly, he came face to face with Marc, Ren, and his parents. All their faces looked bewildered, and his mom's eyes were brimming with tears.

After a long awkward silence, it was his dad who spoke first, "Uh, want to explain that Son?"

Harley started to say something, but no words formed, and he clamped his mouth shut. He pulled his cap off his head and studied it for a few seconds. It didn't seem any worse for the wear.

Trying to come up with an explanation he looked at his dad, the same old man was standing right behind him.

Then he was gone.

∽ 5 ∾

NOT SO CHEERY CHEERLEADERS

"I'LL SEE YOU tomorrow, Kylie!" Katie closed her locker and flung her backpack over her shoulder.

"Wait, what? Where are you going?" Kylie hurried to catch up.

"My dad's taking me to get my car after school."

"You're so lucky. My dad said I have to drive my mom's car and since she is always in it, I doubt I will ever get to drive."

"Well, it's not a new car. Just one that I can get to work and back in."

"And drive to school?"

"Hmmm! Good idea!"

Katie pushed the heavy double doors open and she and Kylie escaped the confines of high school.

They stopped by the flagpole while Katie searched the parking lot for her dad. She noticed a white-haired old man walking across the parking lot.

"Who do you suppose…"

"Oh wow, here they come." Kylie interrupted her friend and smacked Katie's shoulder.

Katie turned in the direction Kylie was looking.

Yep, here they come—Sami, Gena, and Melissa—all juniors and three of the most popular girls at Westlake High. All three were cheerleaders and dating guys on the football team. Rumor had it they had been friends since kindergarten, and it was obvious that all their families had money.

Gena's parents moved to the other side of the valley when she started high school. She threw such a fit, her dad bought her a brand-new Charger so that she could drive the fifteen miles from home and finish high school with her comrades.

Katie moved in from California just three years earlier and had never really known much about these girls. They had gone to a different middle school than she did so she had no expectations about them one way or the other.

She and Kylie had been friends since the seventh grade and danced together outside of school as well as in the Westlake dance club. Both girls had just made drill team for next spring. Neither of them knew the three girls well enough to even bother saying hi to them in the hall—not that they would give Katie and Kylie the time of day even if they did make the effort. They only knew the girl's names because their reputations were larger than life.

But that had changed last week.

Brennan, Sami's boyfriend, was in Katie's economics class and had made it a point to take a seat near her. He was friendly, ridiculously handsome with jet black hair, clear blue eyes, and was tall and muscular. Katie couldn't help but be flattered by his attention.

That lasted three days and then Joey, one of Katie's friends from church, informed her that Brennan was Sami's property, and she should probably steer clear of his attention.

Katie decided to do just that. She wasn't rude to him, just cool and Brennan had noticed. In fact, just the day before he had confronted her about why she wasn't talking to him in class anymore.

Katie told him she had heard that he and Sami were dating, and she didn't want to get in the middle of that.

"She doesn't own me. Besides, we can be friends, right?" was Brennan's response and Katie had just smiled and nodded.

That was yesterday.

This morning, Kylie heard a rumor that Sami had it in for Katie—and from the looks on the three girls' faces, the rumor appeared to be true.

Katie didn't like confrontation and was basically shy. She just wanted to mind her own business and have fun at school.

The stories of the bullying these girls participated in were well circulated and Katie had often wondered how they got away with it and still stayed on the cheerleading squad. But the reality was, she had never experienced it firsthand.

That, it seemed, was about to change.

Without hesitation, Sami walked directly up to Katie. Even her walk was intimidating. Add to that her tall slender frame and cascading blonde hair, she was a little overpowering.

"So, I hear you're flirting with my boyfriend." Sami planted herself right in front of Katie, one hand on her hip and the other jabbing a finger in the air at Katie's face.

"You heard wrong," muttered Katie.

"That's a lie and you know it," Gena snapped.

"It's not a lie. I don't like your boyfriend." Katie's heart pounded. "He's just in one of my classes."

"The story I'm getting is completely different. I was told you are leaning over his desk—asking him for help—that's what I call flirting."

"Like I said, you heard wrong." Katie turned to walk away.

"Hey!" Sami grabbed Katie's arm.

"Is there a problem here?"

Katie whirled at the sound of her dad's voice. She shrugged Sami's hand off and pushed past the three girls.

"No problem, Dad." She walked briskly toward her dad's car with Kylie on her heels.

Dad did not immediately follow, and Katie turned to see what he was doing.

He was standing there staring after the three girls who must have left in a hurry because they were already inside the school and the doors were closing behind them.

Katie opened the car door and climbed in the front seat. "Do you want a ride, Kylie?"

Both girls looked up to see their bus pulling out of the parking lot.

Kylie sighed, "Will your dad mind?"

"I don't think so."

Right then dad walked up behind Kylie. "Miss your bus?"

"Uh, yeah. I guess I did."

Dad walked around the front of the car toward the drivers' side. "C'mon, I'll take you home."

Kylie climbed in the back seat and Dad steered the car out of the parking lot. "Want to tell me what's going on?"

"Nothing, Dad. Those girls are jerks, I guess. I don't really know them."

"I saw her grab your arm, Katie."

Katie turned to her dad, "thanks for not saying anything."

Dad nodded. "So, I guess you are not going to tell me why she grabbed your arm."

Katie shook her head. "It's nothing."

Dad glanced back at Kylie, and she jumped at the chance to volunteer information.

"That was Sami—she thinks Katie has a crush on her boyfriend, who is totally good looking and on the football team, but that's not it at all. He, Brennan I mean, has a crush on Katie and obviously Sami is jealous," she took a deep breath and then sighed.

Katie rolled her eyes. *I think I will kill her now.*

Dad looked at his daughter, "Is that true?"

"No, it isn't true! I don't like her stupid boyfriend."

"That's not what I asked."

Katie glared at Kylie then turned to her dad. "He talks to me in class, Dad, that's it. She is just a freak."

Dad laughed but he didn't say anything.

"It's this street Mr. Cyla. Third house on the right."

He turned onto the street and pulled to a stop in front of Kylie's house, and she jumped out.

"Thanks! See you tomorrow, Katie! Have fun getting your car!"

Katie smiled and waved, "Yeah, see you tomorrow."

Dad pulled away from the curb. "Are you sure you're, okay?"

Katie nodded, but her stomach was in knots.

"Still want to go get your car?"

She laughed. "Duh, Dad."

"Okay—do you want to talk about this Brennan kid?"

"Nope, there's nothing to talk about."

Katie tried to forget about Sami when they pulled into the car dealership. The little blue car was parked and ready for her to drive home. She had been so excited but as hard as she tried, the incident at school had really put a damper on the moment.

The car was clean and shiny, and the inside smelled like vanilla. She assumed they put one of those freshener things in like her mom used in her car. She climbed in and her heart raced. She had wanted this car for weeks and Mom and Dad had finally come up with a plan for her to help pay for it.

Having her license only a month, Dad was a little concerned about her driving alone, but she assured him she was fine and that she would follow him all the way.

It thrilled Katie to be driving her very own car and when they got home, she took her mom, dad, and her sister for a ride and then after dinner she went to her room to do her homework. The anxiety had still not left her, and she dreaded going to school tomorrow. But she decided to try to forget it. She, Kylie and two of her other friends, Natalie and Lisa were all going to the football game after school, and she had been looking forward to that.

The four girls found seats near the fifty-yard line about halfway up the bleachers. None of them knew much about football, but the excitement in the air made it fun just to be there. This was the girls' first high school football game and Dad had even let her drive her car with the promise she would come straight home after they got something to eat at a fast-food restaurant. Of course, the school was only about two miles away and the fast food only about another two, but she still felt pretty grown up.

She carefully parked checking to make sure she wasn't too close to the two cars next to her, so they wouldn't hit her shiny new doors.

The football team ran onto the field and the girls jumped to their feet cheering and clapping like the rest of the student body.

"Oh my gosh, he's looking right at you!" Kylie grabbed Katie's arm.

"Oh, wow and Sami is looking at *him*," added Natalie.

Kylie was right, Brennan was looking right at her and when he caught her eye he grinned, then turned around and pulled his helmet on.

Katie slowly looked toward the cheerleading squad who were all in a huddle on the track right in front of the bleachers.

Sami, Gena, and Melissa were all staring at her—a better word would be glaring.

Suddenly Katie got mad. "Who does she think she is?"

"Exactly! Who does she think she is?" said Kylie, and Lisa and Natalie agreed.

"I haven't done anything to her and I'm not going to talk to Brennan anymore."

"Question is, will he quit talking to you?" said Natalie.

Katie resolved to move seats in her economics class on Monday.

Westlake won the game by one point with a field goal, and everyone left happy.

On the way to the parking lot the girls laughed and discussed their limited knowledge of football.

Suddenly Katie shrieked and stopped within a few feet of her car. Her three friends stopped with her.

Katie could not believe what she was looking at. Horrible ugly scratches all the way down the side of her car. The scratches were deep into the metal; three distinct gouges starting at the front bumper and running all the way to the back bumper.

Katie couldn't say anything. Tears filled her eyes and her heart felt as though it would burst.

"Those lousy freaking girls!" Natalie screamed and ran to the other side of the little blue car. "Both sides! I can't believe this!"

"Should we call the police?" asked Kylie.

"And tell them what?" Katie was sobbing now. "Who would do this? How would we know what to tell the police?"

"We *know* who did this." said Lisa.

"Do we? Those three were on the field the entire game!" wailed Katie.

"But we didn't see them leave, and we didn't exactly hurry out of the there," said Natalie.

"Yeah, that's true." Katie choked on the words as she punched the button on her keyring and the car doors unlocked.

The four girls climbed in, but Katie didn't start the engine. "What am I going to tell my parents?"

"You didn't do anything," said Natalie.

"I know but…" Katie rubbed her eyes, but she could not stop crying. "My brand-new car."

"Hey Katie, want me to drive?" Kylie had gotten her license over six months ago.

Katie hesitated but then she nodded and opened the door. She and Kylie traded places and Kylie started the engine, but Katie stood outside assessing the damage.

"Holy cow what happened to your car?" It was Joey Sandler, and some kid Katie didn't know.

"I don't know," whimpered Katie.

"Someone keyed it," said Joey's friend.

"Probably that witch Sami," said Joey.

"Would she really do this?" said Katie.

"Wouldn't put it past her. She has been known to do worse," said Joey

His friend chimed in, "Well not her alone but the three of them are psychotic."

"Why hasn't anyone done anything about it?"

Joey looked at Katie and sighed, "Money talks and Sami and Melissa's moms are on the school board."

"So? What difference should that make?"

"It shouldn't," said Joey, "it just seems like it does, that's all."

Right then, a car pulled up behind Katie's car and Gena leaned out of the back window. "Oh wow, did someone scratch your brand-new car?"

Katie glared at Gena. "Yeah, *someone* did."

"Oh waaaaaa…" and the driver sped away.

Suddenly Katie was angry, and her insides were on fire. "I hate her!"

"That's the spirit! We should…." Kylie jumped out of the car followed by Natalie and Lisa.

A loud cawing sound interrupted Kylie and they all looked up.

Lisa screamed, "Look out!"

Katie froze as a huge black crow seemed to be flying right towards her.

"Get down!" yelled Joey as he pulled Katie to the ground.

The massive bird came so close to Katie she felt the wind from its wings as it swooped within inches of her head.

Bewildered, she stood and looked at her friends.

"Where did she go?" Natalie spun in a circle. "Where's Katie?"

"I'm right here," said Katie.

Joey thrust his hand in Katie's direction, hitting her in the face. He jerked back. "What the?"

Katie's hand flew to her wounded cheek, but she did not see her hand in front of her face, and she looked down. She screamed when she could not see her own body, "Where am I?"

"Okay this is freaking me out…" Natalie started to back away.

"What's going on, Katie? We can hear you, but we can't see you," shrieked Lisa.

"*I* can't see me!" Katie started to panic. "I'm gone…I mean my body is gone…I mean I'm still here but…"

"There you are!" Kylie was still standing by the drivers' door, but Natalie, Lisa, Joey, and his friend were at least two parking spaces away by now.

Katie looked down. She squeezed her arms and touched her face. "Yes! I am! I'm right here!"

"Wow…that was very cool." Joey walked back toward Katie, "actually, that was—weird."

Katie's body tingled. She was dizzy, and for a few seconds she leaned against her car. Suddenly, an involuntary surge of energy coursed through her, and she felt empowered, strong, like she could do anything.

Surprised by her own voice and seemingly acceptance of disappearing she said, "Let's go find them!"

"What?" shrieked Natalie, "What if you disappear again?"

"Let's hope I do!" Katie jumped into the front seat and closed the door and her three friends climbed back in as well.

Joey was running to his truck with his friend on his heels, "We're coming too!"

Kylie sped out of the parking lot, but Katie didn't care that she was driving so fast. She had a new-found confidence—right this second, nothing scared her.

Natalie leaned up from the back seat. "Aren't any of you the least bit concerned that Katie disappears?"

"Katie doesn't seem to mind," said Lisa and pulled Natalie back into her seat. "Put your seatbelt on."

Natalie looked sideways at her friend, "okay but this makes no sense at all."

Katie glanced at Natalie, "I don't know what it is—it doesn't hurt—and it may not stay around, so I'm going to take advantage of it while I can."

"Doing what?" asked Lisa.

'You'll see." Katie didn't look back at her friends, she stared straight ahead.

"I think it's awesome," Kylie laughed, "they're always at Kneaders. Let's go there first."

Kylie was spot on. The car Gena had leaned out of was parked right in front of the entrance to the restaurant.

"Do you need some keys?" asked Natalie.

"What?" Katie looked at her friend but then she realized what Natalie meant. "Oh! No, I'm not going to do that. I have a better idea."

Katie closed her eyes and thought of the bird. "Can you see me?"

"Uh, yes," said Kylie flatly.

"Oh, hmmm." But just then the three girls came out of the restaurant and headed toward the car. Katie felt the same surge of energy again and she looked down. Sure enough, she could not see her legs.

"Uh oh…you're gone again. What the…?" said Natalie but Katie did not wait for anyone else. She threw the car door open and jumped out.

She ran directly toward the three girls and the first thing she did was grab Sami's purse and toss it under their car.

Sami screamed at her friends, "Why did you do that?"

"Do what?" Gena's look of surprise made Katie laugh.

"One of you took my purse!"

Gena and Melissa exchanged a confused look and then they both turned to Sami.

Katie reached up and pulled the clip out of Sami's hair and then flipped it over her head, so her hair was covering her face.

Sami pushed the hair out of her face. "Knock it off you guys!"

But Gena and Melissa simply stared at their friend.

Katie pushed Sami backwards until she was against the door of the restaurant. By now Sami was crying. "What is happening to me?"

Katie let go of Sami and ran to Kylie and snatched the car keys from her hand. She then ran around her own car to the car the girls were driving. She held the keys by the side of the car as though she was going to scratch it.

Sami stared at the keys moving through the air. "No! That's my dad's car!"

"Who are you talking to?" Melissa's brown eyes now were wide as saucers. "Sami you've lost it!"

"Are you telling me you can't see those keys?" wailed Sami. She clapped her hands to the sides of her head. "Who are you?" she screamed.

Katie was again right in front of Sami, but she did not touch her. She leaned in close and whispered in Sami's ear, "Your worst nightmare."

Katie walked away, leaving Sami crying and embarrassed in front of her two friends and half the football team that had gathered in the parking lot.

I'm not sure what this is, but I like it.

Katie started toward her three friends. Just before she opened the car door, she saw that same old man standing near the door of the restaurant. He was looking directly at her. For a few seconds she stared back.

"Katie, get in."

Responding to her friend, she opened the door and leaned down, coming."

She looked back to the old man. He was gone.

He can see me when no one else can.

She hesitated, thinking he might come back, but he didn't. She slid into the seat and pulled the door shut. Her friends were staring in her direction, but she knew they couldn't see her.

She grinned, "Let's go eat."

~ 6 ~

No Place for Real Guns

Nate stared at the ceiling. He attributed the reason he couldn't sleep to his excitement about tomorrows Air Soft game, and the fact that he would be using his two new guns for the first time since Christmas.

But he knew that wasn't all it was.

He rolled over on his side and stared out the window. His gaze drifted to the Nessumsar coat of arms hanging on his wall. Drawn to it, he sat up. He studied it closely for several seconds and then he remembered—the dream.

For months he had been dreaming the same dream and it had awakened him again tonight. In the dream he was a Viking, and when he wore those clothes, he was invincible. Maybe it was because his dad had been talking to him about their Viking heritage since he was a little boy. He wasn't sure—all he knew is that the dreams invaded his sleep night after night, and he didn't know what they meant.

There was an old white-haired man in his dream. Who was he?

If anybody or anything—maybe they are just dreams.

But they sure seemed like something more. If so, what?

Nate climbed out of bed, walked near his door, and lifted his newest gun from the menagerie. A Colt M4 CQB Full Metal RIS Rifle with 2 Mags. This was going to level the playing field. The team they were up against were professionals—semi pro—and they had agreed to meet Nate's team this Saturday for two games as a special favor for Nate's upcoming sixteenth birthday.

This promised to be a competition of all time for Nate's team, and he had hardly been able to contain his excitement.

But now this stupid dream had disturbed his much-needed rest and he couldn't get back to sleep.

He sat on his bed and laid the coveted rifle across his legs. He inspected the barrel and then the magazine chamber. He jumped up and grabbed his vest. Good, both magazines were still in the pouch where he had left them. He carefully placed the vest back on the floor next to his boots.

Nate had checked and re-checked his gear at least a dozen times last night. There was no way he could forget anything. Everything was neatly laid out next to his door for the early morning departing time to meet his team and make the thirty-minute drive to the battlefield.

He trudged up the stairs to the kitchen for a drink of water. Drinking the full glass straight down, he leaned on the counter and narrowed his eyes to read the clock on the microwave.

One am. Sheesh. I should be asleep.

Placing the glass softly in the sink he turned to go back down to his room.

"Nate?"

Nate whirled in a full circle.

"What—who…who said that?"

But there was nothing.

Nate hurried back to his room—not even taking time to go to the bathroom. He would just have to hold it till morning. He closed his bedroom door and dived into his bed pulling the covers up to his chin.

Without moving his head, he scanned the room looking as far in each direction as his eyes would allow. Everything in his room looked exactly like it always did. He shivered involuntarily and pulled the covers even closer to his chin.

"Nate?"

"What?!" Nate sat up nearly bumping his dad's head.

Dad laughed, "What's wrong with you?"

"Noth...nothing."

"I thought you'd be awake by now."

Nate threw the covers off and jumped out of bed. "What time is it? I must have slept in!"

Dad put his hand on Nate's shoulder and pushed him back down on the bed.

"Relax. It's only seven—we have an hour before we have to leave. I just meant I'm surprised you're still in bed. You usually get up at six even when you aren't doing anything important."

"Oh, yeah I know. I couldn't go to sleep last night—you know—too excited. Guess I finally did, though."

Dad was already halfway out of Nate's room. "No problem. You need to eat something though, so best get moving."

"Okay." Nate rubbed his eyes with his fists and then shook his head causing his blonde locks to cover his eyes. He pushed his hair back with his hand and sighed.

What a strange night.

The twelve boys could hardly contain their excitement when they piled out of three vehicles. After collecting their gear, they stood quietly surmising the playing field. Five acres of scattered trees, bushes, rolling hills, abandoned buildings and cars.

Nate turned to his best friend and grinned. Looking just as pleased as Nate felt, Jake grinned back.

"This is so cool." Jake pulled his rifle up to his shoulder and leaned into the gun. Pretending to squeeze the trigger he swung the barrel from one side of the field to the other and back again.

Nate laughed. He could see the other team about fifty yards across the field.

The leader of the other team motioned to Nate, and he stepped away from his friends and joined him about halfway between both teams.

"I'm David." The opponent extended his hand and Nate accepted his quick handshake.

"Nate."

"You guys up for this?"

Nate smiled, "Definitely."

"Not nervous?"

"Nope—well yes." And both boys laughed.

The Olympus Raiders were a semi pro team of mostly college age guys, that hosted games every other weekend at one of four fields in Utah.

"But" explained David, "this is our favorite. It has more barricades than most and I like the hills. They make for a pretty challenging game."

Nate nodded confidently. He didn't want to let on that he really was nervous to battle this team for the first time.

"Well guess we better…" but David stopped talking and Nate turned to see what he was looking at.

Another player dressed in full gear like the rest of them was standing alone about twenty feet behind Nate. It seemed odd that the guy was already wearing his helmet.

Nate turned back to David, "One of yours?"

David shook his head. "No—not anymore. That's Justin. I'm not sure why he's here."

"Do you need to go talk to him?"

David shook his head. "Nope. He won't bother us. He's just trying to make a statement, that's all."

"About what?"

David looked directly into Nate's eyes. "We had to kick him off the team. He was actually our captain."

"And now he's mad that you are?"

"Sort of. There's more to it than that," David shrugged. "No matter. Let's get started."

"Okay—we're ready."

Nate shook hands with the older boy again and they both motioned for their own teams to join them.

David introduced his team and then Nate did the same. Then David laid out the rules of the game.

"Your gun safeties stay engaged until all players have their goggles on. Number two, hands, or gun in the air means, hold your fire. Use this if you don't want to pause the whole game, but maybe your goggles have fogged up and you need to wipe them off—something like that."

David pointed to an area near an old storage container. "Rule number three—safe zone is over there. All players who are out, or need to reload, stay in the safe zone. You cannot fire into or through the safe zone and you can be in the safe zone without goggles. Number four, one hit and you're out for that round. Remember to stay with and defend your team."

"First game, Assassination—Nate and I are the captains, so we will be the objects of the assassinations and whichever team wins that game will choose the subject of Manhunt from the other team. I'll blow this whistle to start the game. Any objections?"

Everyone shook their heads.

"Nope," called one of the Raiders, "let's get this show on the road!"

Nate's hands were sweating. He tucked his gloves in his belt but dropped one of them on the ground. He wiped his hand on his pants and then bent over to pick up the glove

"Nate, look out!" Jake yelled and pushed Nate to the ground.

Nate looked over his shoulder just as a huge black bird swooped toward him barely missing his head and then it darted straight up. Nate scrambled to his feet and sheltered his eyes with his hand to better see the bird. But it was now only a black dot.

"Holy smoke! That thing dang near hit you," said Jake.

"Yeah, dude, are you okay?" David stared wide-eyed at Nate.

"That was close," said Jerry, another of his teammates.

Nate hadn't had a chance to answer any of them when Colin, a boy on the Raiders approached Nate. "Here, I was just putting my phone away and I got a picture," He scrolled the face of his camera and then tapped the screen. "Well, that's strange."

"What?" and Nate and the others leaned in to see the phone.

"The bird was right on top of your head when I took the picture, but there is no bird," said Colin.

"It took off pretty fast," said Jake.

Colin shook his head. "Not that fast and besides, I looked at the picture after I took it. The bird was in the picture. In fact, I couldn't see the back of Nate's head, that's how close the bird was to him."

No one said anything for a few seconds.

Nate shrugged involuntarily, "I'm okay. Let's get started," and he unconsciously scanned the sky.

"Weird," mumbled Jake, as he followed Nate and his teammates to their starting positions.

Nate hurried away from everyone and found cover behind a clump of bushes. As he started to crouch down, he noticed Justin, the banished Olympus Raider, sitting on a rock where he had a vantage viewpoint of the field.

Creepy.

The game had been going on for about an hour. Nate's team had given him great protection throughout, but now they were down to just four players and the Olympus Raiders down to three.

Nate and Jake, along with teammate Randy, had decided to move in for the kill. Their fourth player, Cory, was positioned up ahead where he could direct his teammates toward David who was holed up somewhere near an old, abandoned car, his two surviving teammates keeping guard.

Cory held his two fingers close to his eyes and then pointed in the direction of the abandoned car. Nate knew that meant the enemy was in sight. He crouched down and waited.

Suddenly, Cory clenched his fist and pumped it up and down near his head, time to move forward and fast. With Jake and Randy as point guards for Nate, the three ran in the direction of the car.

Rapid fire took Jake out leaving Nate and Randy on their own.

They took cover and looked to Cory for a signal.

Nate saw David dart from behind the car and at that same instant Cory covered his eyes and then pointed at David.

Ambush!

Nate, Randy, and Cory opened fire and ran directly toward David who stumbled and hit the ground. They weren't sure which one of them hit David, but he was down, and he raised his gun.

In seconds, all members of both teams ran from the bushes, Nate's team cheering as they came.

Nate was shocked. They had won! They chose David to be the object of the manhunt to give him the chance to redeem himself.

After a fifteen-minute break David took his weapons and started off on his ten-minute head start.

Nate finished off a bottle of water and ate the last of his jerky. His hands were tingling, and he wasn't sure what was causing it. He rubbed them together. It wasn't even cold—or hot—it didn't make any sense.

"Ready for another one?" he said to Jake.

Jake looked behind him and then spun around.

"What's wrong with you?" asked Nate.

"Uh—where are you? I can hear you, but I can't…wait…Nate? Is that you?"

"Are you an idiot, of course it's me. I'm right here." Nate reached for his gun but when he touched it—the gun became a sword. He dropped it and it clattered to the ground.

Jake's eyes were as big as saucers, and he backed slowly away from Nate.

Nate's combat boots now were laced and reached his knees. His camouflage pants replaced by dark blue tights.

Tights?!

Each wrist boasted a wide gold arm band and a tunic hung just above his thighs.

I'm wearing a skirt?!

Mortified, he grabbed the cape that now hung from his shoulders with one hand and with the other reached for his helmet that now felt unusually heavy. Something stabbed his palm, and he pulled the helmet off his head. In his hand he held a Viking helmet complete with brass horns.

Nate looked up at Jake who was standing about five feet away staring as though Nate was a ghost.

"What's happening to me?"

Jake shook his head, "I have no idea. But a second ago I couldn't even see you."

Suddenly nausea swept over Nate, and he was back in his combat clothes. His gun lay on the ground where the sword had been.

Jake laughed nervously. "Great trick. How did you do that?"

"You guys coming or not?" It was Cory yelling at them from up ahead.

"Coming!" called Jake. "C'mon, we'll talk about that later," and he took off.

Nate nodded. "Yeah, okay." He started to follow Jake but immediately the nausea returned. He looked at his gun fearful it may turn into a sword again, but instead he could not see his gun, his hands, or his arms! None of him! He was invisible again!

Nate's heart pounded. *What's going on?!*

He heard a noise behind him and turned around to see Justin, the banished Raider, walking right toward him.

He doesn't even see me.

Nate quietly stepped out of the way so Justin would not bump into him.

I wonder if I even take up any space.

He squeezed his arm. Yes, he could feel it.

Justin looked angry. He stopped just before he reached Nate and pulled his helmet off. He reached in his pocket and pulled out a full magazine.

What's he doing? He isn't even playing the game.

Justin sat down on a rock. He clicked a magazine from the chamber of his gun and loaded the full one. He rubbed his face and Nate noticed beads of sweat dripping from Justin's temples.

Nate looked more closely at the gun Justin was holding. It

looked much like his own, but then Nate realized, Justin was carrying a real rifle—the tip had been painted orange to look like an airsoft gun.

"This is your last hurrah old Davey boy," mumbled Justin.

The manhunt had started but Nate did not hear any shots indicating no one had located David yet.

Justin stood up, pulled his mask on, and started to walk in the direction of the game.

Knowing he had to stop him, Nate jumped in front of Justin who bumped into the invisible Nate and then scurried backward.

Startled, Justin looked around him. "What th...?"

Nate visualized the Viking he had been earlier and in seconds with a sword in his hand he faced the surprised Justin.

"Put the gun down."

Terrified, Justin scrambled backward, but the Viking Nate walked deliberately toward the confused boy. He pulled Justin's gun from his hand and giving the signal of distress—fired three rapid shots in the air. He then grabbed Justin by the arm and held him so that he could not run. But Justin did not even try to run—his blank eyes stared at Nate.

Nausea swept over Nate again and he noticed the gold armband on his arm begin to fade. He shook his head and tried to focus on his combat gear.

In minutes, all players from both teams were next to the two boys.

"What's going on up here?"

Nate turned to face David and the others.

Please don't be a Viking.

He must have looked normal because no one looked at him like he was strange—except of course Jake—who peered at Nate from the back of the group.

Nate looked over at Colin. "Hey, you have your phone, right?"

Colin nodded.

Suddenly, Nate was distracted by someone in the trees who stepped into a clearing. *The old man from my dream?*

"And..?" said Colin.

Nate shook his head, now the old man was gone. He felt more confusion but said, "Uh, we better call the police." He clicked the chamber on Justin's gun and the magazine fell to the ground. He then tossed the gun to David. "That's a real rifle. This guy was planning something other than airsoft today."

David stared at the rifle. He looked at his former friend. "Seriously, Justin?"

But Justin just scoffed and turned his head.

Nate's entire body began tingling. He pushed Justin toward David, "Hey I'll be right back." And he ran from the group into a clump of trees.

He was a Viking again.

"This is the coolest thing on the planet!"

Nate spun around. Jake was standing right behind him.

For a second Nate said nothing. His dreams flashed through his mind. What all of this meant, he didn't know. He would talk to his dad—but not today.

Nate wielded the sword in front of him and grinned at his friend. "Yeah actually—it is."

∽ 7 ∾

CRAZY MIND GAMES

His lungs burning, Samual rounded the last corner and headed into the final stretch. This race was twice as long as he usually ran—a full 400 meters at a dead sprint. His legs felt like rubber and his mouth longed for a drink of water.

Students from three opposing Middle Schools were on his heels but he wasn't worried about them. His main competition was the runner just a few feet in front of him. Samual didn't know his name and it didn't matter. All that mattered is that that kid was the only person in the district who had any hope of beating Samual's teammate Jerald. Now it was Samual's job to win this race not only for Jerald, but for their entire team. Their two teams were tied for the District Championship and this race would determine the winner today.

It had been four months since Jerald's family had been hit head on by a pickup truck just before turning off the main road toward their house. The driver of the other car had a seizure, and his car crossed the intersection plowing into the car Jerald's dad was driving. The impact pushed the car into the one right behind them, spun them around, and they were hit again by another car before other drivers could either stop or get out of the way.

Jerald's parents, two sisters and Jerald were all in critical condition from the accident, Jerald suffering two broken legs. The accident had a ripple effect that reached all the way to the Middle School track team. They had counted on winning this year and Jerald was the ticket to winning the 400. None of the other boys could run as fast as Jerald who had trained specifically for this race.

This was Coach Remington's last year and the team wanted to win the District Championship for him.

All seemed to be lost and Coach had taken it in stride. The important thing—he had said—was that Jerald and his family survived. There were a lot of more important things than winning a race.

Samual's teammates understood and agreed with that. But it wasn't Coach Remington who had convinced Samual that he needed to step up to the plate. It was the conversation Samual had with Jerald that had convinced him this was something he had to do.

The entire team had walked to the nearby hospital to visit Jerald. When it was time for them to leave Jerald asked Samual if he would stay a little longer. There was something Jerald wanted to talk to him about.

"I know coach is okay with us not taking first this year, but I'm not," Jerald had said.

"Well, you're not in a good position to make that decision." Being the newest member of the team, Samual hardly knew Jerald, but what he had said could not be disputed.

Jerald had agreed, "You're right—I'm not but you are."

"*Me?!*" Samual had been caught off guard, "are you crazy?"

"Maybe, but I've seen you run. You're fast. You only started last year and already you regularly win the 100 and 200 races. I believe you can win the 400 too."

Puzzled by this statement, Samual stared at his teammate. Only two weeks since the accident, Jerald looked miserable. Both of his legs were in full casts to his hips and his arm and chest still wrapped in bandages. His legs were elevated, and it appeared the only clothing Jerald wore wasn't clothing at all, but a sheet that covered his necessary parts.

"What makes you think I can win the 400? That's twice the distance."

"I told you, you're fast. I've watched you. I was actually a little worried you might decide to run the 400 in training and kick me out of first place."

At that, Samual had laughed right out loud. "Are you kidding me? I could never beat you."

But Jerald did not laugh with him.

Samual stopped laughing and raised his eyebrows, "You're serious, aren't you?"

"Dead serious."

"Samual!"

Samual heard Coach Remington over his own thoughts and snapped back to reality and the fact that he was within inches of the first-place runner.

He was stunned to see his coach running on the infield alongside him.

"You can do this Samual! You got this!"

Samual felt a surge of power from deep within his gut, "I *can* do this."

Jerald's confidence in him and now his coach gave him the extra boost he needed right at that second. His head was spinning—his legs and lungs were on fire but now, he too knew he could win this race.

Samual looked past the runner in front of him—he looked past the finish line—and he ran with everything he had or didn't have. He wasn't sure, but he found it and in seconds he plowed through the tape beating the other runner by centimeters.

He was startled to see and old white-haired man right in front of him.

Samual stopped suddenly, *can't anyone see this guy?*

'You won.'

The man said it, or so it seemed. Coughing and dazed, Samual was scooped up in the arms of his coach and teammates. He glanced back. The old man was gone.

Freezing water doused his entire body as he was hoisted onto the shoulders of his celebrating teammates.

He saw his family on the sidelines hugging and cheering for him. But then the cheering subsided, and his friends lowered him to the ground. They parted, and he came face to face with Jerald who was being pushed toward him in a wheelchair.

Jerald extended his hand and through his tears he congratulated Samual.

"I told you." Was all Jerald could manage to say.

Samual grinned, "Thanks for having confidence in me."

The two boys were swallowed up by their teammates and moved to the grass with the other teams waiting for the awards ceremony to start.

Samual couldn't remember ever feeling as happy as he did when standing on that first-place block. Just as his coach draped the award around his neck, everyone's attention turned to a loud cawing sound directly above them.

Samual looked up just in time to see a huge black crow diving directly at him. He and the others ducked and jumped from the blocks, but the massive bird swooped so close to Samual, he felt the sting of its wing on the back of his head.

Samual grabbed his head and then looked at his hand. There was no blood. "How did that bird not fall out of the sky hitting an object like that?"

His best friend, Connor, was nearby, "No clue but that was crazy. Are you, okay?"

Samual nodded and searched for the bird. It was high in the sky now. Samual could see nothing but a black dot. His entire body tingled, and he felt nauseous. He put his head down hoping to alleviate the nausea but immediately stood back up. *Am I wearing army gear?*

He looked at his arms—sure enough, he was wearing an army jacket. But then, as quickly as it had appeared it was gone.

Samual shook his head. "What was…?"

Connor slapped Samual on the shoulder. "Wow. Guess that crow didn't want you to win." said Connor.

Samual laughed nervously, "Yeah what's up with that?"

Samual's team won the district overall, and after the meet Coach Remington treated the entire team to all the pizza and soda they could eat—it had been a fun and rewarding day for Samual.

Back home, he stood in the shower letting the hot water run down his back. He knew he was pushing it because with five kids they were only allowed ten-minute showers, but so far no one knocked on the door.

Mom must be cutting me some slack, what with my new-found stardom and all.

"I heard that!" Mom called as she passed the closed bathroom door.

"What?" he thought for a second. "Did I say something?" But he knew he hadn't.

Humph—it's a mom thing, I guess.

Samual was surprised his legs didn't hurt too much. He expected much worse tonight considering they had felt like they were tied in knots when he finished the race. Still caught up in the glory of the day he pulled on his sweats, tucked his medal in his pocket and left the bathroom.

He passed his brother on the stairs who whistled and said, "There's the champ!"

Normally Samual would have taken that sarcastically coming from his older brother but this time he knew it was sincere and he grinned.

He laughed to himself. *I never would have believed this day could happen when I joined the track team.*

"I wouldn't have either, but it's so cool that you did it!" said his brother.

Samual spun around, "What?"

"You said you never would have believed this day would happen." His brother looked puzzled.

"I didn't say anything."

His brother scowled, "Oh, okay. Are you still a little dazed because you did say that?"

Samual's eyes narrowed, and he studied his brother's face. He shrugged, "Maybe I did. I must have been mumbling."

His brother disappeared into the kitchen but called over his shoulder, "No, you said it loud and clear."

Samual continued downstairs to the family room. His mom was cooking dinner, his dad had taken the younger kids to the store and his older brother was upstairs. He had the family room to himself. Normally he would pull out some video games, but not today. He retrieved the gold medallion from his sweats pocket and rubbed his fingers across the face of it. To Samual it was beautiful. *I'll treasure this forever.*

"You should treasure it—we are all very proud of you, Samual." Mom was carrying a basket of clothes into the laundry room.

Samual jumped. "Mom, how did you know I thought that?! I didn't say anything."

"Yes, you did, you said you would treasure this forever."

Samual stood. "I think I am going crazy. You guys can hear what I'm thinking!"

Mom laughed. "That's ridiculous. I can't hear what you're thinking. I can hear what you're *saying.*"

Totally confused now Samual went to his room. He got dressed and picked up his cell phone. He had not intended to go anywhere the rest of the day but now he wanted to talk to Connor. He picked up his phone and sent him a text. Connor answered immediately.

"Mom, I'm going to ride with Connor for a while. Is that okay?" Samual called to his mother.

Mom poked her head around the corner and looked up the stairs at Samual, "Aren't you tired?"

Samual shrugged, "No, not much anyway."

Mom laughed, "Okay but only for an hour. I want you home for dinner."

"I'm not hungry."

"Be home for dinner, Dad has a surprise for you."

"Okay." He hurried out the door. He should have been excited for the surprise, but he was trying to figure out why his brother and his mom could hear what he was thinking. He jumped on his bike and sped toward the corner where he and Connor always met.

"So, what's so urgent?" Connor skidded his bike to a stop.

"Come over here." Samual pushed his bike to the sidewalk and the two boys walked into the field and sat down on the dirt.

"Something is wrong with me."

"What? You just won the district track meet for us—what could possibly be wrong?"

"I mean—okay—I'm going to think something, and you see if you can tell what I'm thinking."

"What?"

"Just try it, okay?"

Connor shrugged, "Okay."

Let's go get some ice cream.

"First of all, why do you want to go get ice cream now? And second if you want me to *read your mind,* quit talking."

Samual jumped to his feet. "See! I wasn't talking! That's my point! I was *thinking* that, and you heard me!"

"Whatever, you've lost it. Has that new fame left you wacky in the head?"

"Connor I—okay let's try this. Look right at me." Samual plopped back down on the ground.

Connor narrowed his eyes and stated the obvious, "Okay, looking right at you."

My mom said my dad has a surprise for me.

"That's cool. Any idea what it might…?" Connor stopped and stared at his friend.

"See! I didn't say anything, but you heard me!"

Connor stared at him. His blank expression made Samual laugh.

Samual punched Connor's shoulder. "Am I right?"

Connor nodded slowly. "Try it again."

I hope my surprise is that new hundred and fifty-dollar pair of running shoes I have been wanting.

"The Asics or the Nikes?" Now Connor jumped up. "Whoa! How are you doing that?! And how did you change into army gear?"

Samual looked down. "I have no idea!"

The two boys stared at each other and suddenly, realization hit them both at the same time.

"The crow?" they said in unison.

"Maybe," said Samual, "but how could that be?"

"Who knows, maybe it was an alien. So, uhh, you're in your regular clothes again. This is freaky, Samual."

"I know, I know. But now *you* have lost it. I'm not an alien. It will probably be gone by tomorrow."

Connor nodded. "Just don't think any more today, okay? It's confusing. And—and quit changing clothes on me."

Samual tried to make light of it. "I'll try not to."

"Are you going to tell your parents?"

"No, I don't think so." He shrugged. "Let's go get ice cream."

The two boys rode to the 7-Eleven and Samual tried to consciously think of only ice cream. It seemed to work, Connor said nothing about what Samual was thinking.

They each filled a large cup with both of their favorite, chocolate marshmallow, and stood in line for the cashier.

'I need to wait till that guy isn't looking.'

Samaul turned around to see who was talking. A girl about his age was standing near the candy. She was holding two candy bars near her pocket, and he realized she was thinking about stealing them.

What? I heard her thoughts.

He watched the girl for a few more minutes. She was nervous and fidgeting. He decided to try his new talent on her. He looked directly at her.

Don't do it. Get out of the store before you get in to trouble.

"Did you say something?" Connor eyed him suspiciously. "Dude your clothes have changed again."

Samual noticed a couple giving him odd looks.

That kid must like his fatigues.

Samual looked right at them, "I do. They are kind of hot though, so I change a lot."

The couple looked even more puzzled, and the man moved the woman behind him.

"What? Who are you talking to?"

He grinned at his friend. "Nothing," whispered Samual, and he tried not to look at his clothes.

The girl with the candy bars now looked up and quickly scanned everyone in the store.

Samual turned away from her and pretended to be looking at a magazine in front of him.

Suddenly, the girl dropped the candy bars and hurried out of the store.

Samual grinned and took a huge bite of ice cream. When they were out of the store, he looked at his friend, "This thought stuff could be a cool thing."

"Yeah, but you do realize the army gear you keep changing into looks totally authentic," said Connor.

Samual shrugged, "Uh—I hadn't noticed. I can't figure this out."

"Well, it's all good as long as no one gets suspicious—and if you don't want to keep any secrets," said Connor.

Samual nodded. *Yeah, there is always that.*

He and Connor both laughed.

Samual chuckled to himself, he knew it was kind of mean but he couldn't resist, so he thought, '*there's Peggy Clauson.*'

Connor whirled around, "Where?"

Samual burst out laughing, "Nowhere, Dude, I just wanted to see if you heard me."

Connor glared at his friend, "Okay, not funny. My heart is still racing."

They stared at each other for a few seconds and then both burst into laughter.

"This could be fun," said Samual.

Connor grimaced, "Yeah, I think so too."

Samual tossed his ice cream container into the trash and picked up his bike. "Sorry, I won't do that again. This'll be our secret."

Connor nodded, "Sounds like a plan."

Both boys jumped on their bikes and headed down the sidewalk. Samual looked up at the sky, *this is cool.*

There he was, the old man, almost in the clouds. Samual was not sure why his presence didn't alarm him, but he would worry about that later. Right now, he needed to figure out how not to let his parents hear his thoughts if he didn't get the shoes he was hoping for.

❧ 8 ☙

GO BULLY SOMEONE ELSE

SPENCER PULLED his helmet off—guzzled an entire bottle of Gatorade, pulled a towel out of his football bag, and wiped his face and neck. The California fall had been unusually warm, and it was no exception today.

"Nessumsar!!"

When he heard his last name, Spencer turned in response to his coach and started toward him.

Coach Stewart held up his hand and Spencer stopped but then caught the keys his coach tossed to him.

"Will you go to my truck and grab that grey gear bag? I left it on the back seat."

Spencer nodded. He turned, coming face to face with an old white-haired man. He stopped, but then the man was gone. Spencer shook his head and trotted towards the street where the truck was parked.

Maybe I did get a concussion when I bumped my head.

He passed a group of kids near the trees. There was a lot of commotion coming from their direction.

Spencer recognized some of the kids from school—but not all of them. The two boys he did know, he made a point to steer clear of at school and he did the same today.

The two boys played football but in a different league than

Spencer. They thought they were the coolest guys on the planet and had no problem letting everyone know it. Truth was, they were both complete jerks—bullies.

The first was Tad, big, burly, and freakishly tall for his age. Only in the eighth grade, he was easily six four. It wouldn't be an issue in a bad way if Tad didn't make it one. But he used his mass to push people around, and he usually picked on guys half his size.

Spencer had never had a first-hand encounter with Tad, but Kyle, who was Spencer's best friend, had been bullied by Tad many times. A grade ahead of them in school, Tad had made Kyle's last two years of elementary school miserable every chance he got. If not at school—it would be at the skate park, or the movie theatre, or the grocery store. Any place Tad ran into Kyle when his parents weren't around, he would insult, ridicule or in some way confront Kyle.

Spencer wasn't sure why he was not an object of Tad's bullying. Not that he was complaining, but it did seem odd. He and Kyle were both half the size of Tad, and Spencer figured Tad would single him out as well, but he didn't. Spencer instead found himself being the lookout for Kyle whenever they went any place together, which was nearly all the time, and between the two of them, they had figured out how to dodge Tad most of the time, but it didn't always happen that way.

Spencer felt the familiar anxiety creep into his chest as he passed the group, and he sighed with relief when he made it to the truck without an encounter. He grabbed the bag, locked the door, and turned back toward the field only to come face to face with Tad and his partner in crime, Mike.

"What's up Spencer?" Tad grinned and planted both of his tree trunk legs and massive feet in front of Spencer.

"Not much," Spencer mumbled and attempted to side-step Tad.

"You coach's little errand boy today?" Mike was a full head shorter than Tad but just as obnoxious and he was no scrawny kid by any means. His stocky build, fire red hair, and freckles only added to his intimidating presence.

Surprised that the two bullies were even talking to him Spencer gave them both a puzzled look.

"Practicing football. Just like the two of you." Spencer continued to move around Tad.

"Well, your team wouldn't be able to survive against us," Tad roared.

"Don't think that will be a problem. We never play you," said Spencer, amazed at himself for engaging in conversation. He kept walking slowly, usually by now he would have put a safe distance between himself and these guys.

He glanced in the direction of his team. The second scrimmage team was still on the field. His dad was busy coaching and Coach Stewart had his back to him.

Run!

Even though he thought it, Spencer did not move any faster.

Suddenly, Tad lunged toward Spencer grabbing his arm, but just as he did, something behind Spencer must have caught Tad's attention because he quickly let go and jumped backward.

Instinctively Spencer whirled around. A huge black crow was flying directly at him. Spencer started to raise the gear bag to protect his head, but at that second the crow changed direction and shot straight into the air, having come within inches of Spencer's face.

Mike yelled, "Where did it go?"

"Up there." Spencer pointed into the air as the crow disappeared behind some clouds high in the sky.

Both Tad and Mike whirled—spun in a complete circle to look behind them to where Spencer now realized he was standing, having no idea how he got there.

"That bag is floating!" yelled Tad.

Spencer was puzzled now. He looked down at the bag in his hand—it was floating, and he could not see the entire bag—just part of it.

For that matter, Spencer could not see his hand or his arm, his feet, or his body! He dropped the bag and it landed with a thump on the ground.

"What the…?" yelled Tad.

For a split-second, Spencer found he liked hearing fear in Tad's voice, but he hurried toward them suddenly finding that he was now past them. He turned around and the two boys screeched to a stop.

"What are you doing Nessumsar?" Mike was screaming now.

Spencer looked down—he could see his body again which meant, apparently, they could too.

Spencer took a deep breath. He had to say something. He knew the ball was in his court and this was the first time *ever* he had control of any conversation with these two guys.

"I'm not doing anything. I was just going back to the field." Though shaking uncontrollably inside, Spencer nonchalantly walked past Tad and Mike and picked up the bag.

His entire body tingled, and his heart was pounding so hard he could barely breathe. He had no idea what had just happened, but he also had no intention of letting either Tad or Mike know that he was as confused as they were.

Without another word and without looking back, Spencer jogged back to the practice field. He started to hand the bag to Coach Stewart who asked him to get the game plan book out of the side zipper.

Spencer dropped the bag on the ground, knelt and took hold of the zipper, only to realize he could not see his hand. He quickly took the book out and laid it on top of the bag and then stood and backed away, quickly moving to the other side of his coach.

"Nessumsar?" Coach Stewart looked at the bag and then looked behind him.

Spencer looked at his hands. He could see them again. "Over here, Coach."

Coach Stewart threw him a puzzled look. "What are you…? Never mind, the book?"

"It's on the bag, Coach. I'm…I'm going to get my helmet," and he started toward his own bag and Kyle.

"Yeah okay." Without looking at Spencer, Coach Stewart picked up the book and began leafing through it.

"Saw you over there with the jerks. What did they want?" Kyle walked toward Spencer and handed him his helmet.

"Same as always. Just being themselves—idiots."

Kyle shrugged. "Wish they would die."

Spencer raised his eyebrows. "Die?"

"Yep."

"You don't mean that."

Kyle scowled. "Yes, I do. I hate the thought of going to school with those guys again this fall."

Spencer nodded. "Yeah, me too." He looked back to where Tad and Mike had rejoined the group of kids by the trees. He shuddered.

What just happened?

He searched the sky and tried to locate the black crow. Nothing. Before putting on his helmet Spencer rubbed his eyes.

"You, okay?" asked Kyle.

Spencer turned to his friend as he pulled his helmet over his head. He started to put his mouth guard in place but stopped, "Yeah...I am...I just..." He shrugged and pushed the molded plastic in his mouth and fastened his chin strap.

"What?" Kyle wrinkled his brows.

"Nothing." mumbled Spencer, and at the call for first scrimmage team both boys jogged onto the field.

Toward the end of practice, Dad pulled Spencer aside. "Could you and Kyle do me a favor?"

"Sure, Dad."

"Mom left about an hour ago to run home and pick up the snacks she left on the kitchen counter. She just called and has a flat tire. She is stuck down the street from our place."

"Okay," said Spencer. "What do you want us to do?"

"Your sister has another half hour to practice. Would you and Kyle wait here while I go change Mom's tire?"

"I'm hungry."

Dad sighed. "I know." He glanced at the team. "So is everyone else. That's why your mom went home."

"Can't she call Triple A?"

Dad glared at Spencer. "I'm going to pretend you didn't say that."

Spencer shrugged suddenly feeling foolish. "Sorry."

Dad rolled his eyes. "It will just be till your sister finishes. We'll probably be back by the time her practice is over."

"No problem." Spencer turned to Kyle. "You okay with that."

Kyle laughed, "What choice do I have. I rode with you."

They both laughed and so did Dad.

"Okay, thanks. I'll be right back." Dad pointed to the field closest to the street, "she's right over there."

Anxiety rushed into Spencer's chest as he realized his sister was playing within a few feet of the trees where Tad and Mike had been. He quickly glanced in that direction and was relieved to see that the group of kids had gone.

He and Kyle dragged themselves over to the sidelines of his sister's practice field and both reclined on the ground using their bags as pillows. Spencer closed his eyes and pulled the bill of his hat down for a shield. He may have dozed off for a few seconds, he wasn't sure. But he was sure when he was wide awake again.

"Hey! How did you do that?"

Spencer's eyes jerked open when he heard Kyle shriek. He started to answer Kyle, but stopped when he saw the look on his friend's face. Quickly, he glanced down at his body. Nothing. He was invisible again! He sat up quickly, and looking over his shoulder, he saw what had prompted Kyle's outburst.

Spencer's ball cap had settled to the ground. But before Spencer sat up, it must have appeared to be balanced on the edge of the bag when Kyle could not see Spencer's body. Now with his head no longer holding the hat in place, it fell to the ground.

Why didn't my hat disappear like the rest of my clothes? Wait a minute? Why am I disappearing at all?!

Spencer started to hyperventilate. He leaned forward suddenly realizing he could see his hands again.

He turned quickly to face his friend.

All the color had drained from Kyle's face, and he stared wide-eyed at Spencer.

"Uh…I can…no, actually, I can't explain." Spencer jumped to his feet.

Kyle still sat on the ground, his eyes wide as saucers now. He still said nothing.

The two boys stared at each other.

Finally, when Kyle spoke, he bellowed, "Dude! Are you kidding me?! How did you do that?"

Spencer glared at him. "I have no idea! It's not like I tried to do it!"

"Well try!"

"What? No…why…no…it's weird."

Kyle looked around them. "No one is watching. Try to do it again."

"I—I don't have a clue how to…" but he was distracted by fighting coming from the direction of the trees.

"Leave him alone, Tad! You are such a jerk!"

Spencer knew that voice. It was Sierra Melrose, a girl from school. Her best friend was Chung Nguyen, a scrawny kid who lived in Spencer's neighborhood. Sierra and Chung had been pals since the first grade. It didn't take a genius to know what Tad and Mike were doing. They were not happy unless they were picking on someone. Seemed since they had not had success with Spencer, Chung was now their next victim.

The mild tingling had never left Spencer's body since his encounter with the crow, but now it intensified. He turned to Kyle who was simply staring at him.

"What?!"

"Dude you are like, gone." Kyle extended his arm reaching around with his hand. He suddenly pulled it back.

"That was my face," said Spencer.

"This is insane," Kyle hissed.

"Tad! Stop it! C'mon Chung! Let's get out of here!" Sierra yelled.

But Tad only chortled, "Run home to mommy! Hurry! Hide behind your girlfriend!"

Suddenly, Spencer had an idea, "C'mon." He grabbed Kyle's shoulder.

Kyle stared at his arm as the invisible Spencer pulled him toward the trees.

"What are you doing?" demanded Kyle.

"Just come with me."

"Well, looky here," yelled Mike. "Looky here, Tad, seems like big brave Kyle is coming to little Chung and Sierra's rescue. We all know Kyle has a thing for Sierra."

Kyle choked as Spencer pulled him closer to the crowd. "What are we doing?" he hissed again only this time through clenched teeth.

"Trust me."

"Oh. Alright, no problem. I can't even see you."

Spencer pushed Kyle right between Chung and Tad.

"Whoa, Mr. Tough guy." Tad lifted both hands and shoved them toward Kyle but before they made contact, Spencer jumped between them and punched Tad in the stomach as hard as he could.

Tad doubled over, but then immediately started to rise again.

Spencer didn't give him time to recover. He clapped Tad's head between his open hands and thrust his knee into Tad's face, leaving him dazed as he fell to the ground.

Mike didn't seem to know what to do when Kyle, who must have gained some courage from Spencer, lunged at Mike. But the sheer size of the boy was too much for Kyle and Mike retaliated by throwing a hard-right punch in Kyle's direction.

Spencer jumped between the two boys, careful not to let Mike's punch find its mark on his own face. He grabbed Mike's arm from the side with both hands and pulled it behind Mike's back, pushing his hand up toward Mike's neck locking his elbow and knowing full well that he was causing excruciating pain to Mike's shoulder.

By this time Tad and come to his senses and was again on his feet.

Spencer let go of Mike, and with speed he did not know he had, he climbed up the trunk of a nearby tree and scrambled out onto the branch above Tad's head. Balancing himself by hanging onto two smaller branches, Spencer hurled himself at Tad landing on his back. He wrapped both arms around Tad's neck and hung on for dear life as Tad spun in circles trying to free himself from the invisible vise.

Seeming completely confused, Tad yelled, "Get off me you creep!"

"What creep?" Kyle yelled back, "who are you talking to?"

Tad glared at Kyle. "It's your stupid friend. Get him off me!"

Kyle roared with laughter, but at that second, Mike again lunged at Kyle. This time it was Sierra and Chung, and some kid Spencer did not recognize who stopped Mike. Sierra jumped on his back and the two boys each took an arm and forced Mike to the ground. Two more kids built much like Chung jumped into the action and sat on Mike's chest. Immobilized, Mike was not going anywhere.

Spencer finally released Tad whose face now wore a look of sheer panic. Tad backed away from the group and then turned and ran across the sidewalk and into the street, finally scaling a wood fence and disappearing into a backyard.

"You can run but you can't hide!" yelled Kyle.

Are you kidding me Mr. Bravo?! Spencer didn't dare say anything out loud because only Kyle knew he was there.

"Hey! What's going on over here? Where's Spencer?"

Spencer froze at the sound of Dad's voice. He suddenly thought of not being invisible. He held his hands in front of him and watched as they miraculously materialized. He quickly stepped up behind his dad.

"Uh, right here, Dad."

Dad slowly turned toward his son but then looked back at Mike who was still held captive by Sierra, Chung and three other kids.

"Let him up," said Dad slowly.

The kids let Mike up and he struggled to his feet. Saying nothing, he sprinted away from the group and followed the same path Tad had just taken.

Dad eyed all of them. "Do I even want to know what just happened here?"

"Uhh...probably not..." began Kyle.

"Nothing, Dad, really, we just finally got the best of those two bullies from school," said Spencer.

Spencer's little sister trotted up to the group holding her football helmet in one hand. "What do you mean *we?*" she laughed.

"Dad, Spencer was nowhere in sight! It was Kyle and those other kids who did all the fighting!"

Kyle started to respond but Spencer grinned and shook his head. There was that old man again, right behind his dad.

"Hey…" but then old man was gone—again.

Who the heck…? Oh well, kind of cool, this invisible stuff. And he walked up to Kyle throwing his arm around his friend's shoulders.

"Nice job, Kyle! Guess you showed them!"

WHICH CUBE IS WHICH?

GRANT PULLED his football helmet off his sweaty head and stuffed it into his gear bag. Hefting the bag to his shoulder, he walked across the grass toward the parking lot where his mother was waiting.

"We destroyed those guys!" Nathan Finley caught up to Grant.

The two boys laughed and gave each other a high five.

"Yeah, that was one great game—can't wait till the playoffs," said Grant.

"Hey, wannabe brainiacs!"

The two boys looked behind them. Robbie Higgs was jogging toward them. His twin brother, Chance, was on the opposing team that day. Robbie didn't play football, but he was a total math whiz.

Grant sighed, "What do you want, Robbie?"

"I'm just here to tell you two that you may be heroes on the football field, but we'll see how you do in the math competition where it really counts. You need brains not brawn," Robbie chided.

"You're such a jerk, Robbie. You cheat all the time, and you know you do," said Nathan.

"Yeah, too bad you're not more like your brother," said Grant.

"What's that supposed to mean?"

"It means that Chance is a nice guy—too bad you're not more like him," said Grant.

"Great game you guys!" Mom called to them from her SUV. She

already had the back open for the boys to stow their football bags.

"Thanks Mom," said Grant. He turned around and called to Robbie, "See ya in school Monday!" but then he mumbled, "you jerk."

He waited for Nathan to get in the car and glanced again in Robbie's direction. There was an old man with long white hair standing about ten feet away from Grant.

Grant climbed in the back seat after Nathan. "Hey, Mom, do you know that old guy?"

Mom turned to look at Grant, "What old guy?"

"Right…" he pointed in the direction the old man had been, but he was gone.

"Hum, he's gone, never mind." Grant pulled the door handle, but before the door closed, they heard Robbie, "Yeah, you guys are toast!"

"What was that all about?" asked Mom.

Grant rolled his eyes. "That kid is trying to win first place in the math competition."

"Well, so are you guys—so why is that a problem?"

"We just beat his brother's team," said Nathan.

"And…?" Mom looked at them both through the rearview mirror.

"And he always says we have more brains than brawn," said Nathan.

Grant laughed, "More brawn than brains."

Now Nathan laughed, "Oh yeah."

"Maybe he's right." teased Mom.

"Whatever. He's a jerk. His dad always makes some huge donation to the math department, and I'm sure that's why they don't say anything about his cheating," said Grant.

"I guess you two will have to win fair and square," said Mom.

"It's kind of hard when he gets away with everything," Nathan grumbled.

Mom changed the subject. "Today was a great game. Only one more for the championship."

Grant perked up, "Yeah we slaughtered those guys!" He grinned at Nathan and the two boys bumped knuckles.

Mom pulled the SUV to a stop in front of the pizza restaurant. Other members of Grant's football team were also arriving.

"I'll be back in twenty minutes. I have to pick up your brother and sister."

Grant and Nathan jumped out of the SUV.

"Okay, Mom."

"Thanks!" called Nathan, and he slammed the door.

"At least we don't have to listen to Robbie here. The *losers* probably just went home," said Grant.

"Yeah." Said Nathan.

But when the two boys walked into the restaurant, there stood Chance Higgs and several other players from the other team.

Grant groaned, "What are they doing here?"

Nathan shrugged. "Who cares, let's go get some pizza."

Grant followed his friend scanning the restaurant for Robbie but there was no sign of him.

It wasn't that Grant didn't like Chance. It was just his stupid brother. Robbie was always ragging on Grant and Nathan about math and it irritated Grant. He could hold his own against Chance—math came easy to him—but Nathan, smart as he was, always buckled under competition. It was crazy too, because he wasn't like that on the football field, just in the math competitions.

Mom had said once that maybe Nathan felt more comfortable in his football clothes. *'Sometimes just putting on a uniform gives a person a kind of power—not a real physical power'*—Mom had explained—*'but they feel more powerful.'*

Grant had scoffed at that idea. *'I don't think our shorts and blue T-shirts will do the trick.'* He had told his mother.

Grant took a huge bite of pepperoni pizza and chased it down with root beer. This was the best part of football—the eating parties after the games.

After a few minutes of chowing down pizza and breadsticks, Grant's coach stood at the front of the group. About that same time, Mom returned with Grant's little brother and sister. To his chagrin, she was followed by Robbie Higgs and his mother.

Nathan nudged Grant.

Grant grunted, "I see him."

Coach Kimber had a microphone in his hand and began by praising his team and their accomplishments. Grant's chest swelled with pride, as did the rest of his team. They deserved the compliments—they really had played exceptionally well this year.

It was what Coach Kimber said next that shocked Grant. "As you know, Coach Higgs and I are brothers-in-law."

NO, I didn't know! Coach Higgs?????

Coach Kimber continued, "His son, Chance, is one of his best players. This season of football is nearly over—with just one more game to play, and Coach Higgs is behind us all the way to win the championship."

A roar went up from the players on both teams.

"So," continued Coach Kimber, "they will be there to cheer us on," another roar.

"However, earlier today I learned about another competition— one that could mean at least $10,000 in scholarships to a team of two from our own football team."

Suddenly, there were slaps on Grant and Nathan's backs from several of their team members. Most of the kids knew about the competition—it had been going on all year in school. But that is not where Grant's mind was—he was studying rich Mr. Higgs. This was the guy who donated thousands to the math program at their school—and as a result—at least that's what he and Nathan thought—Robbie Higgs always managed to win, even though it was obvious he was cheating.

"Grant?"

Grant was startled out of his thoughts by the sound of his own name booming through the microphone. He stood and followed Nathan to the front amid cheers—and some jeers—from the crowded pizza parlor.

This time it was Coach Higgs, "Robbie? Will you and Chelsea join me?"

Now Grant thought he was going to die. Robbie's math competition teammate was Chelsea Hintze—she and Robbie were in the same class. How could Grant not know this minor little fact? His heart pounded inside his chest when Chelsea joined them—he'd had a crush on her since the 4th grade.

I hate my life.

Grant saw his mom. She was cheering and clapping along with the rest of them, but the look in her eyes told Grant she knew what he was thinking. It had always been impossible to keep things from Mom.

Coach Kimber continued in his zeal, "I understand these four students will be representing your school at the state competition in two weeks. Let's all give them our support and may the best man—or woman—win!"

Another rambunctious roar from the room and after smiling at Chelsea and scowling at Robbie—Grant made his way through the crowd to his mother.

"Can we leave?"

Mom put her arm around him. "We can if you want, but this is your football party. Why don't you stay and play the games for an hour?"

Grant's eyebrows furrowed and he sighed a huge deep sigh. "Coach Kimber just ruined the party."

"We can leave if you want to, Grant."

Just then a tug on Grant's arm pulled him away from his mom. "C'mon Grant, we're playing some video games."

It was Chelsea, and Grant simply grinned at his mom as he was swallowed up in the crowd.

Over two hours later Mom pulled the SUV into the carport and the family piled out.

"Grant, could you push those trash cans out for the garbage truck?"

"Sure." Grant dropped his gear bag at his feet and walked slowly to the cans near the garage door. He was in the alley behind his house—the roar of the ocean just a hundred yards away.

He pulled one can out and reached for the other. Just then a huge black crow landed on the can.

Grant froze.

The crow was the biggest bird Grant had ever seen—except for that one annoying pelican several weeks ago. This bird was far from annoying—this black bird was scary.

Its steely green eyes were fixed on Grant's blue eyes—Grant was afraid to move, but the thought occurred to him, *do crows have green eyes?*

Suddenly the crow lunged at Grant, but just before hitting him it darted straight up and disappeared into the night sky.

Immediately Grant let go of the trash can leaving it where it stood, grabbed his gear bag, and ran inside the garage locking the door behind him. He ran into the house. "Mom!"

"I'm upstairs."

Grant dropped his bag again and took the stairs two at a time.

"Mom there is a huge black bird outside."

"Grant there are a lot of birds around here."

"Yeah, but this one was…"

Mom looked at him curiously now.

Grant sighed, "Yeah, it was just a bird."

Mom laughed. "You've had a long day. Time for bed."

Grant couldn't argue with that. It had been a great day and the worst day all rolled into one. After his shower, he crawled into bed and tried not to think about Robbie Higgs or his dad, or the big bird. His thoughts drifted to Chelsea Hintze and then he was asleep.

The entire next week Grant and Nathan prepared for the math competition. Their teacher, Miss Braithwaite had the other students take turns drilling the two boys on different aspects that they would be challenged with. It was hard for them both, but especially for Nathan. He knew the answers, but he got frustrated under pressure.

"Nathan you can do this. You know the answers."

Nathan shrugged. "I wish I could not think about the other people. It's easier in our classroom."

Just pretend you're alone.

Nathan looked up. "What?"

Grant scrunched his face, "I didn't say anything."

Nathan shrugged.

"I was just thinking you could pretend you're all by yourself. Like maybe in your bedroom."

"Yeah, that's what you said before," said Nathan.

"I didn't…. never mind," Grant shrugged.

He's losing it.

"I am not losing it."

Grant stared at his friend. "How did you know I was thinking that?"

Nathan shrugged. "I don't know. Were you?"

Grant nodded. Then he thought of the ocean and pictured Nathan sitting on the sand by himself answering the math questions.

Nathan grinned. "This is cool. I can remember everything when I'm alone."

"Holy cow!" Grant jumped to his feet.

"What?"

"Nothing, nothing. But we're going to win this competition!"

"What about cheating Robbie Higgs. It won't matter how much we know—he'll win. He always does."

"Leave Robbie Higgs—and his dad—to me." Grant grinned. He was not sure how this was happening, but he decided to test it on some other kids.

After eating their lunches Grant and Nathan joined some other classmates to play soccer.

Chelsea was standing by the drinking fountain talking to two other girls.

Grant stared at all three of them. He pictured in his mind Chelsea walking along the beach with him. He wasn't sure it worked until suddenly Chelsea looked directly at him and smiled and then she nodded.

Grant's eyes widened. Did she really *see* what he was thinking? He had to know.

Grant called to Nathan, "See you inside!" and he jogged right toward Chelsea. He slowed down just as he reached her and her two friends.

"Hey Chelsea."

Chelsea blushed, "We should take a walk on the beach sometime."

Grant nearly fell over. All he could do was nod his head and grin. Suddenly, he felt foolish, and he hurried past her into the school.

Friday came all too soon, and Grant found himself perched on a chair in the middle of the school cafeteria along with Nathan, Chelsea, and Robbie. Today would determine which team would go to the state math competition and have a chance at the $10,000 scholarships.

Each of the four chairs had the competitors names on them and all four students were decked out in blue T-shirts and white shorts—just like Grant had told his mom. The chairs were positioned in a wide half circle so the four could see each other easily.

Miss Braithwaite and Mr. Chambers, and Chelsea and Robbie's teacher, along with the principal were sitting at a table facing the four students. They each had a microphone.

Grant looked over at Robbie who simply glared at him and Nathan.

Chelsea squirmed in her seat and Grant wondered if she had to go the bathroom.

Nathan looked nervous.

Grant hadn't even told his mom about his new mind control stuff. He decided to try it out on Nathan right now. He stared at Nathan and thought of birds singing…no, he didn't want to think of birds…instead he thought of trees and grass and a soft breeze.

A soft smile crossed Nathan's lips and almost immediately Grant thought he looked more relaxed.

Grant smiled. He had no intention of using his mind control talents on Robbie—but—he would if he had to. Robbie always managed to cheat, and the other students couldn't understand why he never got caught.

The competition began. The first round went rather easily. All four students answered the questions without hesitation leaving the two teams tied.

The next part of the competition involved solving a Rubik's cube. The cubes had been scrambled before the competition and the winner would be the team with the fastest time. Each team had to complete three separate cubes and teammates could help each other if they needed to.

When the principal said go, the four students expertly twisted the colored cubes. Grant noticed Nathan's hands start to shake uncontrollably. He looked at Nathan.

You are in your bedroom playing with the Rubik's cube.

Nathan stopped twisting the cube and simply stared at it and Grant's heart dropped. Maybe Nathan wouldn't finish it at all.

Nathan began slowly turning the colored cube this way and that and then suddenly produced the completed cube amid cheers from the entire audience.

Grant hurried to finish his and now the two of them worked on the third cube. He glanced over at Chelsea and Robbie. She was trying to complete the puzzle when Robbie suddenly grabbed it from her hands, dropping it from the table. It landed in Robbie's open backpack.

Immediately Robbie retrieved it from the bag and placed it on the table in front of him. He twisted it once and produced the completed cube exactly at the same time Grant and Nathan completed theirs.

Chelsea scowled at Robbie, but only Grant seemed to notice— he also noticed the smirk on Robbie's face.

Hmm, I wonder....

The two teams were still tied.

Grant looked over at Coach Higgs who was smiling confidently at his son.

The last part involved difficult math equations. A large white-board was rolled onto the floor and Miss Braithwaite and Mr. Chambers each stood holding black dry erase markers. This was the hardest part of the competition. The teachers would take turns writing one at a time a total of six different problems on the white board. The students were to write their answers on their own smaller lap white boards and then hold them up for the teachers to see.

The first two problems were hard but not impossible, and all four of the students scored 100%.

The third one posed more of a challenge and all four students seemed to struggle with the answer, but then suddenly Robbie held his board up. His answer was correct—the other three did not complete the equation in the allotted time, putting Robbie and Chelsea in the lead.

Grant looked over at Robbie. He kept reaching up and scratching his neck. *What's wrong with him?*

Grant turned to look at Coach Higgs. He seemed to be talking to himself because no one was standing near him.

The next problem was on the board taking Grant's attention away from Robbie and his dad.

This problem was even harder than the last one and Grant had to concentrate to work through it. But it wasn't long before he and Nathan both had the answer. Chelsea too held her board up, but Robbie seemed to be struggling. He kept scratching his neck.

Grant looked at Coach Higgs and then back to Robbie. Grant was sure he knew what was going on. He stared at Coach Higgs.

The answer is the number five.

Coach Higgs was still talking to himself.

Grant looked over at Robbie who was scribbling something on his whiteboard. He looked nervous and unsure of what he was writing. Suddenly he dropped his marker and thrust the board in front of him.

A collective gasp escaped the entire audience.

Robbie had written a huge number 5 on his whiteboard.

Even Miss Braithwaite and Mr. Chambers seemed flustered

by Robbie's answer. It was nowhere near the correct answer and Miss Braithwaite stuttered when she announced the three correct answers were from Chelsea, Nathan, and Grant.

Grant stared at Mr. Chambers.

Ask Robbie what's in his backpack.

Grant was surprised to see the same old man he had seen at the football field, standing by the gymnasium door.

Mr. Chambers suddenly stood and casually walked across the floor to where Robbie sat. He leaned down close to Robbie and said something to him.

At first, it appeared that Robbie was protesting, but then he dropped his head, leaned over, and pulled a Rubik's cube from his backpack.

Grant looked back toward the old man. He was gone.

Now it was obvious what had happened. Robbie had the completed, correct Rubik's cube in his backpack. When he seemed to accidently drop the cube he was working on, he replaced it with the finished one.

Mr. Chambers did not look happy. He said something else to Robbie, and after a few minutes, Robbie pulled something from his shirt and handed it to Mr. Chambers.

Without saying anything, Mr. Chambers guided Robbie to the table and said something to the principal. The principal took Robbie with him, spoke briefly to Coach Higgs and the three left the room.

Even if Robbie hadn't been disqualified, Grant and Nathan still won the chance to go to the state competition to compete for the $10,000 scholarships.

"Congratulations, brainiacs." Mom laughed when the boys were presented the winning trophies.

Grant felt kind of bad for Chelsea, but she didn't seem to care too much.

"I hate math," she confessed.

It was several days before anyone knew what had happened with Robbie and his dad. The truth was, Robbie simply did not know the answers, so Coach Higgs had rigged a little speaker in Robbie's shirt, so he could tell Robbie the answers. It was his idea to put the Rubik's cube in Robbie's backpack too.

Grant wondered if anything would happen to Coach Higgs and Robbie, but Mom said the humiliation was probably enough punishment for them.

A few days later Grant and Nathan were leaving football practice.

"That was so weird at the math competition. I wonder how Mr. Chambers knew what was going on."

Grant shrugged. "I don't know. Maybe it was magic."

Nathan eyed his friend. "Do you think…no, that's lame."

Grant grinned, "You never know."

∽ 10 ∼

INVISIBLE SUPPORT

"Good job, Kitana! You nailed it that time!" Coach Simmons called and Kitana looked over at him and grinned.

She had been practicing that dismount from the beam for weeks. She needed to score high to place in the top three in an upcoming meet against their toughest competitor, The Flyers.

Kitana skipped off the mats to her bag and fumbled through it for her water bottle. She sighed when she saw it was nearly empty.

Her friend and teammate, Demi, was standing nearby. Kitana called to her, "Hey, want to go fill our water bottles?"

Demi shrugged, picked hers up and joined Kitana. They walked in silence for several seconds.

"Finally got your dismount, huh? Good job," Demi said flatly.

Kitana started to respond but was interrupted by Jessie and Geraldine as they clamored down the steps near the drinking fountain. All four of the girls had been on the Tags Gymnastic Team for two years.

When they saw Kitana and Demi, Jessie said, "You're such a loser, Demi. How do you think you can possibly place on Saturday without your uneven routine?"

"Yeah, gymnastics is a four-event sport Demi. Not three!" laughed Geraldine.

"Leave her alone." Kitana glared at the two girls and walked past them. Just as she did, an old man with pure white hair walked toward them. She stared at him for a few seconds, but then she turned her attention back to her teammates.

"You have nothing to worry about, Kitana, but Demi is going to bring our team score down."

Kitana glanced at Demi whose eyes were brimming with tears. She quickly put her arm across Demi's shoulders and pulled her past the two girls.

"You guys worry about you; Demi will be just fine," snapped Kitana.

"Yeah, whatever," said Jessie. "I'm surprised coach hasn't kicked her off the team."

"He probably will before Saturday." Said Geraldine.

"Why are you two so mean?" Kitana whirled around to face the two girls. "Does it thrill you to make other people sad?"

"She just needs to know the truth, obviously you won't tell her," Jessie laughed and pulled on Geraldine's arm, "c'mon."

The two girls disappeared into the gym and Kitana turned to Demi.

"It's the truth, Kitana. I can't get it. I have really tried, but I can't seem to pull my Kip to the high bar and my dismount is the worst." Demi started to cry.

Kitana hated seeing her friend like this. They were not only teammates but also best friends. Demi's fears were real. She had fallen off the bars a year ago and broken her ankle. She had been having trouble with the bar routines since then.

"Maybe I can help. We could stay after and practice."

"I *have* practiced. I can do it if I know a spot is there, but as soon as coach is gone, I freeze up and miss it every time. What's the use?"

Kitana thought for a few seconds. "The use is, that you can do it. You've done it before. I know you can!"

Demi shook her head, "I don't know, Kitana, I have been thinking of quitting. I just don't want to do that to my mom. This has been a huge sacrifice for her to keep me in gymnastics since my dad died. I know it would disappoint her if I quit."

Kitana's eyes narrowed. "You're not going to quit. We'll work together. You *will* get this!"

Demi smiled through her tears. "I'm glad you think so."

"I know so." Kitana drank some of her water. "C'mon, let's go talk to coach."

Coach Monserrat was very encouraging and gave Kitana and Demi the go ahead to practice for an extra two hours by coming in early. It was summer, so school was not a problem. He even offered to stay with them for an extra hour after team practice. But when Demi went to call her mom to tell her Kitana and she were staying later, the coach pulled Kitana aside.

"I appreciate your efforts, Kitana, but I am not sure this is going to work. Demi has had trouble with the bars since her accident. She simply psyches herself out."

"I know, I know, but we have to try. I think she can do it. She just needs to build her confidence."

Coach Monserat smiled. "She has five days, Kitana. Five days. That's not much time."

Kitana nodded. "I know."

The hour practice after team did not help much. Kitana could see the problem. When Demi flew off the bars a year earlier, she had been attempting to transfer from the high to the low bar, but she had too much speed and literally flew away from the bar, across the crash pad and hit the gym floor. She landed on her left ankle, shattering it. Now, every time she had to release the bar, she panicked and dropped to the floor. If Coach Monserat was there to spot her, Demi could execute the move seamlessly, but as soon as she was alone, she couldn't do it. Saturday's meet was an elite competition, spotters were not an option.

That night Kitana did not sleep much. When she woke up the next morning, she pulled on her sweats and running shoes and went outside for a short run. She needed to clear her head. Since she was a little girl, she had been particularly sensitive to other people's feelings and now, at twelve, it seemed to only be intensified with her desire to help her friend. Not only for the team, not only for Demi, but if Kitana was honest with herself, she wanted to show stupid Jessie and Geraldine. They were two of the brattiest girls she had ever met. They weren't really team players at all; they were all about their own glory.

The next two days proved almost futile in Kitana's efforts to help Demi overcome her fear of releasing the bar. Coach Monserat had demonstrated the spotting technique he used for Demi so that Kitana could do the same. Kitana was not as tall or as strong as the coach, but that wasn't an issue since the coach never even touched Demi. He was just there for moral support.

At first, Demi did not have the same confidence in Kitana as she had in her coach—it was no wonder, Kitana had never spotted Demi or anyone else for that matter in this difficult routine.

Kitana was starting to wonder if this was a good idea, but then coach suggested something.

"Kitana stand where I am, and I will stand over here." Coach Monserat moved about three feet away from Kitana. He then turned to Demi. "Okay, do your routine. I am close enough that if I see you struggling, I can step in, but you will know that Kitana is there for you as well. If nothing else, she can break your fall."

"Gee thanks, Coach," Kitana scowled.

"Well, you know what I mean," he laughed. "Neither of you will die."

"Comforting, isn't he?" Kitana rolled her eyes and Demi laughed nervously.

Demi mounted the bars and did a perfect back hip pullover—then swinging her right leg over the bar, she executed two full 360-degree rotations, pulled to a handstand, and then spun twice around the lower bar. It was right here that she had to release and blindly transfer to the high bar.

For just a second Kitana thought she saw hesitation in Demi's eyes, but she did not break her rhythm. She landed squarely on the high bar with her hands perfectly spaced. Pulling to a handstand she did two 360 degree one-hand rotations and back to a handstand. Now it was time to dismount.

Demi executed two complete rotations to pick up speed—her dismount was to be a full double twist into a layout back tuck, landing facing the bars. Demi did not miss a beat. She executed her dismount with precision and then burst into tears.

"Why are you crying? That was perfect!" Coach held both hands up for a high five from Demi. She reciprocated and then her tears turned to laughter then back to tears again. "It made a difference having you close, coach. I…I need to try it without you nearby."

Their coach grinned. "Well let's do it."

Demi started her routine, but when she was supposed to release, she dropped to the floor.

"What…?"

Demi held her hand up to stop Kitana. "Again, let me try again."

Kitana shrugged and looked at coach who nodded.

This time Demi completed the full routine. It was not quite as smooth as when the coach was close, but never-the-less, she did it.

One day to go. Now it was time for Demi to try it without Coach or Kitana spotting her.

She tried it three times and dropped to the floor every time. The second time she made it to her final dismount, but when she left the high bar, she simply did a handstand forward roll out and popped up on her feet.

That was a move neither Kitana nor Demi had used in years. It was a basic, elementary move young-gymnasts learned early on to escape if they felt they were in trouble. If they caught their error in time, it worked. If not, they pretty much crashed.

***

Again, Kitana did not sleep much. This was the final day, Friday, Demi had to complete the routine by herself. Feeling particularly energetic this morning Kitana ran to the top of the hill she usually ran with her mom. She hadn't planned to, she just did.

While running, she noticed a huge black crow circling above her. It would caw off and on, but it never came close to her. Still, it made her feel a little uneasy. The black bird looked as though it was big enough to carry her away if it wanted to. She had seen lots of birds in this area over the years, but never one this big.

Kitana reached the top of the hill and playfully pumped both fists in the air and jumped up and down like she had seen Sylvester Stallone do in a Rocky movie. She took a long welcome drink from her camelback and dropped to the ground throwing her head back to stretch her neck. She stopped and held perfectly still.

That weird bird was stopped too, right above her. High in the air, but right above her. How in the world was that crow holding perfectly still like that?

The thought occurred to her to run back down the hill and to the safety of her house, but she didn't move. She looked around to see if there was anyone else up here. There wasn't, and she knew her mother would kill her if she knew Kitana had run up this hill by herself. It was not allowed. She was far from home and so high up no one could hear her if she yelled.

Still mesmerized by the complete stillness of the bird, Kitana reached into her pocket and pulled out her cell phone. Full bars. Good, at least she could call for help.

Without taking her eyes from the bird, Kitana slowly started to stand.

Suddenly, the crow began cawing so loud it was deafening and Kitana put her head down and covered her ears with her hands.

The sound of flapping startled her, and she looked up. The bird was diving right for her.

Kitana froze. It seemed to her as though the bird would smash right into her face, but she could not move. Quite sure she was about to meet her demise, Kitana was shocked when the bird, coming within inches of her face, suddenly shot straight back up into the sky.

She fell on her back staring up until the bird became a tiny black dot. Still, she didn't move. She felt for a second as though she was floating and then every nerve in her body seemed to be tingling.

It was several minutes before the feeling subsided and Kitana had presence of mind to sit up. She shielded her eyes and scoured the sky for the mischievous bird.

Nothing.

She struggled to her feet, her legs feeling like rubber, and slowly walked back down the hill and home. She entered the kitchen through the garage door, finding her mom at the kitchen sink.

"Kitana?" Mom turned around and looked straight at her daughter.

Mom looked surprised. "Oh…that was strange. How did that door open? I must not have closed it all the way."

Mom walked across the floor and closed the garage door. She then picked up her cell phone from the table. "I'll give that kid ten more minutes." She placed the phone back on the table and went back to the sink.

Kitana stared after her mother, *What's up with Mom?*

Kitana took her own phone out and plunked it on the table, but she was shocked that she could not see her hand or the phone. The phone became visible only when it touched the table.

Mom spun around, and her eyes widened when she looked at the two cell phones. When she looked toward the garage door again, Kitana grabbed her phone. As soon as it was in her hand again it disappeared.

Kitana's heart was racing. She didn't dare say anything to mom. She already looked like she had seen a ghost! Maybe she had.

Maybe I'm dead! Maybe that crow killed me!

Kitana raced up the stairs, but just as she hit the top landing, her cell phone rang.

Oh no! Mom's calling me. This will be a dead give-away. There is that word dead again. What is happening to me? Why am I hiding from my mom? Well, I'm not actually hiding, not intentionally!

"Kitana! Are you upstairs?" her mom called.

Kitana fumbled for the answer button on her phone. She could see her hand—her arm! She looked down. Her whole body! She leaned over the stair banister.

"Hi, Mom, were you calling me?"

"Yes, when did you come in? How long have you been up there?"

"Just a few minutes—didn't you hear me? I had to hurry, I had to go to the bathroom."

Mom clicked the end button on her phone with her thumb. "Uh…well yes actually I thought I heard the door open."

"Oh, well I'm back! Going to take a shower."

Mom didn't answer, or if she did, Kitana didn't hear her. She hurried into the bathroom and locked the door. She stared at herself in the mirror. Nothing out of the ordinary.

She turned on the shower and started to undress, and then she thought of her narrow escape from the bird. Her body began tingling again and she reached for a towel.

She could feel the towel in her hand, but it seemed to float off the towel rack. As soon as it was clear of the rack the towel disappeared.

Kitana spun around to face the mirror. NOTHING! She was invisible!

What is happening?!

Kitana jumped back crashing into the wall.

Still dazed, she took a quick shower, and by the time she got out, the tingling had stopped, and she could see herself again. She hurried to dress and then called to her mom from her bedroom. "Okay if I go over to Demi's for a little while?"

Mom must have come up the stairs because she was now right outside of Kitana's bedroom door. The knob turned, and Mom appeared in the doorway.

Oh, please be visible!

"It's okay, just be back by noon. We need to run to the mall this afternoon."

Relieved, Kitana nodded.

Mom gave her a questioning look, "Are you okay?"

Kitana nodded vigorously. "Yes! Why wouldn't I be?"

"I'm not sure…did you run up the hill again?"

Kitana felt her face flush. "Yes, I'm sorry."

Mom's voice turned stern now. "Kitana if you keep doing that, I'm not going to let you run by yourself."

"Okay, Mom, I promise I won't. Not ever." Kitana knew she would for sure never go up there alone again, so it was not a hollow promise.

"Okay. I don't want to worry about you. Just stay in the neighborhood."

Kitana nodded. "Okay, well, I'll be back in a while."

"By noon!" Mom called as Kitana ran down the front steps.

She didn't stop until she got to Demi's house, and she banged on the front door.

Demi pulled it open. "Geez are you okay?"

"Demi you have to come with me! I need to show you something."

"Come where?"

"No wait, never mind, can we go up to your room?"

Demi slowly nodded. "Sure, but you're acting kind of weird."

Kitana pushed Demi up the stairs and when they got into Demi's room, she closed the door and locked it. She stood still for a second.

"Is that you, Kitana?" Demi's mother was in the hallway.

"Yes, hi!"

She heard Demi's mother laughing and then go down the stairs.

"What is wrong with you?"

Kitana looked directly at her friend and then past her to her fan. "Turn that on?"

"What?"

"Never mind." Kitana scooted past Demi and turned the fan on high then she turned around to face the bewildered Demi.

"I am going to do something. Don't scream or freak out or anything, okay?"

"I'm already freaking out," laughed Demi.

"Demi, I'm serious!"

Demi held up both hands. "Okay, okay. What?"

"Watch." Kitana closed her eyes and thought of the black crow. Immediately her body started to tingle.

"What the?" Demi gasped and quickly backed up until she bumped into her bed and fell backwards.

Kitana tried to think of something other than the bird before she completely vanished. She thought of the gymnastics meet.

"You were disappearing, Kitana!"

"Yeah, but now I'm here again, right?"

Demi's mouth was wide open, and she slowly nodded. After a few minutes of saying nothing, she narrowed her eyes. "Do it again."

Surprised, Kitana grinned. "Okay."

Once again, she thought of the bird, and again, the tingling, and she began disappearing. This time she became completely invisible.

"You can't see me, right?"

Demi nodded, "Right." She said slowly.

But come here, you can touch me.

Demi did not move.

"Okay fine, I'll come over there."

Demi scrambled onto her bed.

"Demi it's me, I'm right here."

"It might be you, but you are NOT right there."

"I am, give me your hand."

Demi slowly extended her hand and before she could pull it away Kitana grabbed hold of it.

The two girls stood silently and then Demi whispered, "I can't believe this."

"I know, huh? So cool."

"But how?"

Kitana told her friend about her run up the hill and the bird and how it almost hit her and then she became invisible.

"Does it hurt?"

"Nope, not a bit. But my body tingles a lot."

Kitana shook her head—suddenly she was visible again. She grabbed her friend by the shoulders, "Don't you see what this means?"

"No, I guess I don't." Demi's look was total bewilderment.

"I can spot you and no one will know—no one but you!"

"How the heck will I know?"

"I'll tell you. I'll talk to you—but you can't talk back, or everyone will think you're crazy." Kitana laughed.

"Actually, I think I am—and so are you."

"Possibly, but for now this will work. I know it will!"

Saturday afternoon came and the meet against the Flyers was quickly drawing to an end.

The Tags were ahead but not by much, however, Demi and Kitana, Jessica and Geraldine were in the top five along with one girl from the Flyers. Kitana was in the lead and if Demi could execute her uneven routine, she could bump one of the other two out of second place, but the fifth girl had to score under a nine. She was good though, so it would be close.

Demi took her place in front of the uneven parallel bars.

As she did, Kitana saw the same old man. He was standing near the end of the balance beam. He smiled at her, and then he was gone. Kitana stared where he had been for a second. *Who is that?* She glanced around, *can't anyone else see him?*

She shrugged, stood out of sight, and concentrated on the black bird. Just like before her body tingled and she watched as her hands disappeared. When she was fully invisible, she ran to the bars and whispered, "I'm here. You got this."

Demi's routine was flawless, scoring a perfect ten and advancing to second place right behind Kitana. The girl from the Flyers took third, bumping Jessica and Geraldine to fourth and fifth consecutively.

Coach Monserat was beside him-self as he accepted the first-place trophy and draped medals around the girl's necks.

Just before the photographer snapped the victory picture, Jessica called up to Kitana, "I guess miracles do happen."

Kitana laughed, "You have no idea!"

～ 11 ～

STEALING ISN'T COOL

LOCK SAT GLUED to the television screen engrossed in the new Ninja Turtle movie. He had everything imaginable that had to do with Ninja Turtles—all four characters and the playsets to go with them. The movie ended and Lock quickly went up to his room, pulled out his Ninja Turtle action figures and began reenacting the entire movie.

His older brother stood in the door of his room. "You know they aren't real, don't you?"

Lock glared at him. "I know it."

His brother laughed, "okay, just making sure you haven't totally lost your mind."

"Get out of here." Lock stomped across the room and slammed his bedroom door. He heard his brother laugh as he went down the hall.

Lock played for another hour, creating scenarios for each of the turtle action figures to complete daring feats while saving a part of humanity from certain doom.

He was interrupted by a knock on the door.

His mother cracked it open, "Lock dinner is ready, and then you have some reading to do, don't you?"

"Yep, okay."

Lock quickly tucked each of the action figures safely in their storage boxes, cleaned up the accessories and carefully put them away under his bed. Still dressed in his Ninja Turtle pajamas, he hurried downstairs.

After dinner it was his turn to load the dishwasher, but as soon as he finished, he found his backpack and pulled out two books. For school, he had to read a chapter in his history book, so he hurriedly read it, being careful to take note of important things he might need to know for school the next day. Now it was free reading time and he had chosen one of his favorite books, *Ninja Turtles Save the Day*.

Lock loved to imagine himself in every battle, always triumphant in the end. Soon it was time for bed and Lock crawled between his sheets, holding his huge stuffed Ninja Turtle, Michelangelo.

His parents came in to kiss him goodnight and when they left his room, he heard his dad say, "That kid is obsessed."

But Lock didn't care. He knew his dad was right.

'Michelangelo! Run they're after us!' Lock jumped from the top of the car and landed on the back of a motorcycle driven by Leonardo.

Lock looked back as the motorcycle sped away. Michelangelo was running as fast as he could.

'Leonardo, wait, Michelangelo can't catch us.'

Leonardo pulled the motorcycle to the side of the road and stopped, "You wait here."

Lock jumped off the bike and sought cover inside a nearby store. He pressed his nose against the glass door and waited.

Minutes later the two Ninja's sped by him but a second cycle skidded to a stop. It was Donatello who yelled at Lock, 'Get on. Let's get out of here.'

Lock burst through the door and leaped from the sidewalk to the back of the bike grabbing Donatello's belt and holding on for dear life as the cycle sped away.

'I think we've lost them,' yelled Lock. He kept looking back but there was no sign of the black car that had been following them.

Thirty minutes later and a safe distance away, they pulled into a warehouse. Michelangelo and Leonardo were right in front of them, and Raphael stood guard at the door until they were all safely inside.

Michelangelo jumped off the bike and raised his hand, 'High five, Lock, you were awesome out there.'

Lock grinned and returned the high five.

'I think Lock needs to be an honorary Ninja—what about it guys?' said Donatello.

'Agreed,' yelled the other three Ninja Turtles in unison.

Lock was suddenly hoisted into the air and when he turned to see who had lifted him up, it was an old white-haired man.

Lock opened his eyes and rolled over onto his back. He could smell bacon. He sat up quickly and then plopped back down on his bed, "That's right—it's Saturday. No school."

He closed his eyes recalling his dream. Another night spent with the Ninjas, and he smiled.

After breakfast and chores, Mom dropped him off at the skate park with his friends and told him she would pick him up in two hours. He grabbed his skateboard and charged up the hill.

"Wow, there are a lot of people here today!"

Mike was his best friend and was waiting for him. "Yeah, but maybe some of them will leave at lunch."

"I hope so," said Lock.

The two boys dropped their skateboards, jumped on them, and joined other skaters in the crowded park.

"Hey, did you get a new deck?"

Lock glanced back at Mike. "Yep—my dad brought it home from a trip. Pretty cool, huh?"

"It's awesome!"

Lock smiled and glanced down at his new deck, complete with all four Ninja Turtle images.

Lock had been working on his ollie—he still couldn't get it right and his dad had explained that the ollie was the basic of all skateboard tricks, so he had to master it. He was pretty good at rail sliding on curbs, but he hadn't dared try it on a handrail. He had also been working hard on his tail slide. His dad had also made it clear he was not allowed on the half pipe until he mastered those tricks and could keep his balance simply riding on a sidewalk—but *that* he could do almost perfectly.

Lock got frustrated with so many rules, but Dad had been doing this stuff since he was a kid and said he didn't want Lock dead. That always made Lock laugh.

After a while, Lock and Mike sat down on the grass and pulled out their snacks and water. They watched as some of the better skaters executed trick after trick on the half pipe and marveled at their talents.

"See that kid over there?" Mike pointed to a tall dark headed kid on the other side of the park. "That's Jason—he goes to competitions. He has like four decks and all of them cost some major bucks."

Mike directed Lock's attention to the three expensive boards leaning against the fence, "He rides all of them in one day."

"How come?"

"I don't know—I guess he's trying to decide which one he likes the best. That's what my brother says."

Lock shrugged. "Humm." He was distracted by a huge black crow sitting on the branch of a nearby tree. Even more curious, an old white-haired man stood next to the crow. The same old guy as in his dream.

Who is that?

"What are you looking at?"

Lock pointed at the crow. "That bird—look how big it is."

Mike whistled. "Wow—that is one big bird."

Lock nodded. "Do you see the old guy?" He tipped his head back and drank the rest of his water.

"What old…Lock duck!" Mike grabbed his friend by the shoulders and pushed him to the ground.

"What?" But he didn't have to wait for an answer.

The huge crow was headed right for them and both boys buried their faces in the grass.

The bird swooped just above Lock's head and then shot straight into the air.

Lock rolled to his back. "What the heck was that?" He searched the sky but couldn't see the mischievous bird.

A couple of older kids nearby ran toward Lock and Mike.

"Are you guys, okay?" said one of them.

Dazed, Lock nodded, "That was weird."

"That bird almost nailed you," said the other kid.

"Yeah—it—did." Lock looked at Mike who was staring at his friend.

The two kids stood there for a few minutes, and then they walked away leaving Lock and Mike alone again.

"I feel kinda sick," said Lock.

"Probably because you're scared to death!"

"I'm not scared—well okay, maybe a little."

Mike laughed. "It scared me."

Lock rubbed his hands together. His whole body was tingling, and he stood up, "I'll be right back."

Lock started to walk toward the restroom, but suddenly he was at the restroom.

He stood perfectly still trying to figure out how he had traveled the distance from the skate park all the way across the grass to the restroom in an instant—and he couldn't remember doing it.

Feeling nauseas again, he stepped inside the bathroom. The metal mirror above the sink made it hard to see a reflection, but as Lock passed by it, he froze, staring at the fuzzy figure looking back at him. He was looking into the face of a Ninja Turtle—but which one?

Lock spun around to look behind him—there was no one there—he whirled back around—the Ninja stared back at him.

Feeling even sicker, he ran to the sink—threw up and then washed his mouth out. The cold water relieved the nasty taste. He dropped his head and leaned on the sink. He wanted to cry, or call his mom, but his cell phone was in his backpack at the skate park.

"Lock, are you okay?"

Lock raised his head at the sound of Mike's voice. Now looking in the makeshift mirror he saw his own reflection. He quickly turned around to face his friend, "Yeah, now I am."

"How did you do that?"

"Do—do what?"

"Get over here so fast. One second you were standing right next to me and the next second you were gone."

"I—I don't—I don't know. It was weird. It made me sick."

"To run that fast?"

"I didn't run."

"Yes, you did, you were running superfast."

Lock scrunched his eyebrows. "I don't know, Mike. I can't explain it either."

"Do you want to go back and skate?"

Lock nodded, "Yeah."

They walked back to the skate park, and by the time they got back, other than being a little shaky, Lock felt fine.

They picked up their boards, and just as they did, something caught both of their attention.

Two boys were hovering close by where Jason's three boards were leaning against the fence. A third boy was standing on the other side of the fence.

"What are they doing?" said Mike.

"I'm not sure." Lock looked around the park until he found Jason. He was paying no attention to the boys or his boards.

"Lock, they're stealing those boards!" yelled Mike.

Without thinking, Lock ran toward the boys—in an instant he was standing on the other side of the fence, and he snatched one of the boards from the third boy, who had just been handed it across the fence.

The boy started to pull the board away, but suddenly stopped cold and stared at Lock. "What are you doing? Are you like in costume or something?"

Lock said nothing. The kid was inches taller, but Lock grabbed him by the front of his shirt and lifted him off the ground.

"I don't know what you're talking about, but I know you're stealing Jason's boards—now put them back."

Without letting the boy down, Lock slowly turned to look at the other two boys—they were staring at him with their mouths and eyes wide open.

"Uh, Lock?"

"What?" Lock's voice sounded lower than usual. He looked at his friend—Mike's expression was the same as the three boys.

Lock let go of the kids' shirt, who then dropped to the ground, but he didn't move.

Now Lock realized everyone at the skate park was staring at him. No one was saying anything—in fact the silence was deafening.

"Are you—like—are you a Ninja Turtle?" whispered Mike.

"What? No—no I'm not."

"Yes, you are—but which one?" said the kid on the ground.

Lock scanned all the people's faces and then turned to Mike, "I'm just Lock."

"Lock the Ninja you mean," said a girl standing close by but Lock couldn't see her.

The crowd burst into cheers and clapping.

Embarrassed, and not knowing what else to do, Lock picked up the three boards and walked over to Jason, "Here, I think these are yours."

Jason slowly nodded, "Yeah—they are. Thanks, man."

Lock nodded, "No problem."

He turned then and walked over to Mike. He could feel all eyes watching him and he wanted to get out of there fast.

Lock picked up his board and his backpack. "Meet you at the

snack bar," he whispered to Mike and with that, he was gone.

Lock stood in front of the snack bar—the girl was just opening the roll up door. "Hi!" she said when she saw Lock. "I'll be open in a few minutes."

Panting, Mike joined him. "How do you run so fast? Hey, you're not a Ninja anymore."

Lock looked down—he was wearing his jeans, T-shirt, and converse tennis shoes. He grinned at his friend. "I don't know what happened to me—but it was awesome."

Mike laughed, "Must have been that stupid bird."

Lock scanned the sky but there was no sign of the bird. "Yeah, it must have been." He turned his attention back to the snack bar where the girl was waiting for his order. He glanced at Mike who was counting one-dollar bills in his hand.

Lock sighed.

I hope that bird comes back

DON'T MESS WITH MY BEST FRIEND!

MRS. GILBERTSON passed out the test papers to her third-grade class and then went back to her desk. Before she sat in her chair she said, "As soon as you are finished you may go to recess."

Noelle scanned the test paper. *Hmmm, this doesn't look too hard.*

She glanced across the room to see if Mollie had started the test. She had, she was writing madly and didn't notice Noelle. Both girls had two of their favorite Monster High dolls in their backpacks—Mrs. Gilbertson had told the class the day before that they would get an extra-long recess today after their tests were complete. But Noelle also knew that it was possible to use the entire recess on the test and that would ruin the girls plans.

Noelle and Mollie usually did not bring their Monster High dolls to school—but this was a special occasion. Both Noelle and her best friend had received two brand new dolls for Christmas, and they were eager to play with them. Mrs. Gilbertson's tradition was to invite her students to bring a toy from home sometime in the first week after the Christmas holiday and today was that day.

Soon, the first student finished the test and quietly left the classroom. Within minutes several other students, including Mollie, also finished.

Noelle's heart started beating faster—she glanced up when Mollie paused at the door to look back at her.

Mollie cupped both hands around her mouth, "Hurry up." She didn't say it out loud, but Noelle could read her lips and she nodded.

One more problem—Noelle flipped the paper over to the other side and her heart sank, *ugh, I hate story problems!*

She read it over and over, but she kept glancing at the clock watching the minutes tick by. She rubbed her damp palms on her new skirt and then tried to concentrate on the problem, but she couldn't focus—time was running out.

She had even dressed special for today—pink printed Monster High leggings, high top shoes with the Monster High insignia, a ruffled black skirt that had little wisps of silver running through the fabric, a pink and blue long-sleeved shirt with Monster High plastered across the front and matching pink and blue ribbons adorning each of her long pigtails.

She tried to focus on the story problem centered around rockets, some kid named James and another one identified as Billy. She was sure the fact that Billy Cummins sat behind her in class and constantly tormented her made it even more difficult for her to sort out this math problem. However, she had noticed earlier that Billy wasn't even in class today so that couldn't be it. Still, she decided that he was *usually* there and that was causing her to have a lack of concentration.

Noelle knew that wasn't true. She simply wanted to get out of this class and go to recess.

"Noelle?"

She hadn't noticed her teacher standing next to her.

"Ye…yes, Mrs. Gilbertson."

Her teacher placed a finger on the paper—she slowly moved her finger to another part of the problem. "Think of it this way—you and Mollie each have two new dolls—but you need to add Ginger's two and Samantha's one. Now put those together—then take away one of Ginger's because she forgot it today—how many dolls does that leave?"

Noelle scribbled on her scratch paper, 2 + 2 + 2 + 1 = 7—1 = 6

Six!" said Noelle. She looked up at her teacher who simply smiled and walked back to her desk.

Noelle quickly wrote the answer on her paper—scooped up her backpack and hurried to place the test paper on Mrs. Gilbertson's desk.

"Wow, thanks Mrs. Gilbertson. That was so much easier than rockets," *and stupid Billy Cummins.*

Mrs. Gilbertson laughed as Noelle ran out of the classroom. She hurried down the hallway pulling the backpack shoulder straps into place so that she could run more freely, but careful to slow down when she passed open classroom doors, lest a teacher see her and order her to walk. She burst through the double doors that lead to the playground and started toward the pre-designated spot she and Mollie had decided to meet.

But Mollie wasn't there.

Maybe Mollie went to the park. I hope not—we'll be in trouble.

The park near the community swimming pool was adjacent to the school playground but students were strictly forbidden to play in the park during school. It was not a part of the school property and took the students out of the protective eye of the playground monitor.

The girls' meeting place was in a clump of trees right on the border between that school and the park. They knew they had to stay within view of the playground monitor, but it was also far enough away from the other kids that they could play undisturbed with their new dolls.

Noelle ran toward the trees. She saw an old man with long white hair on the other side of the playground. He was standing next the playground monitor. She thought it was weird he was there, but maybe he was someone's grandpa.

When Noelle reached the tree where the two girls were to meet, she found Mollie's open backpack and one of her dolls, lying on the brown winter grass. She knew that was not like Mollie—she would never treat her doll like that.

Noelle looked around. A little farther away she thought she saw Mollie's jacket and she ran to it knowing she had now overstepped the boundary. She glanced back, the playground monitor was breaking up a fight between two boys and did not appear to have seen Noelle.

Suddenly, Noelle heard a muffled scream—she looked in the direction she thought it came from, and to her horror, she saw Mollie in the front seat of a car Noelle did not recognize.

Mollie was pounding the window with her fist and screaming something. This time Noelle could not read her lips, but she knew immediately what was happening—Mollie was being kidnapped!

She heard the bell ring, and now giving no thought to her Monster High dolls, Noelle shed the backpack and it dropped to the ground.

Noelle turned and started to run toward the playground. In that same instant she heard a loud cawing above her head, and she looked up. A huge black bird was flying directly at her.

Noelle ducked and covered her head with both hands, but the bird swooped within inches of her, and Noelle crashed to the pavement scraping her hands and knees. She heard the flapping of the bird's massive wings, but when she looked up the bird was high in the sky and barely visible.

Her heart pounding, Noelle scrambled to her feet. Her entire body was tingling, and she wondered if the bird had hit her or if she felt that way because she had fallen.

She looked toward the parking lot again just as the car that held Mollie prisoner started to pull out onto the street—but it had to stop for a fire truck and an ambulance, both with sirens blaring.

Noelle didn't know what to do. The playground was empty. She knew if she went in the school, she would lose sight of the car, but then she realized she would anyway because it was driving away. The fire truck and ambulance passed, and the car started moving again. Without thinking, she ran toward the car—she knew she needed to remember what it looked like to tell her teacher.

"Noelle!"

She looked back when she heard her name. Miss Jensen, the playground monitor was yelling at her. But Noelle didn't stop—she pointed in the direction of the parking lot and screamed, "Mollie is in that car!"

She didn't know if Miss Jensen heard her or not, but she didn't dare stop—she had to keep her eye on that car.

She could see that it was blue, and it had only two doors. She tried to see if there was something different about that car than other blue cars because she didn't know what kind it was. Just before it turned the corner, she found what she was looking for—five stick figures in the back window. The familiar stickers in people's windows usually represented the family that owned the car.

Tears streamed down Noelle's face as the blue car stealing her best friend turned the corner and disappeared out of sight. Suddenly, she felt a surge of energy course through her entire body. She looked down at her new skirt that she had torn when she had fallen—her new leggings had holes in both knees and the scrapes on her hands burned. She pictured Mollie screaming and pounding on the window and she cried harder.

Noelle started running again, only this time she ran so fast that she covered the parking lot in seconds. She jumped over a curb, and when she did, her entire body lifted off the ground—she kept running until she realized she didn't need to run anymore—she was flying!

She didn't try to figure out how she was flying, she kept going and flew toward the street where the blue car had gone. People below her screamed or yelled and pointed at her, but she kept going. The car had turned onto the main street but was nowhere in sight. There were two ways it could go to get to the freeway and Noelle figured that would be where the driver would go for a fast getaway. To get a better view of the ground and the streets, she flew higher into the sky. Now she could see the freeway in both directions as well as the road that went over the freeway leading to a shopping center.

For a second, Noelle panicked. There were so many cars on the freeway. How would she find the blue one?

She heard sirens. Two police cars were speeding down the main road—they each took one of the two roads to the freeway—one going north and the other going south.

But Noelle had a different idea—maybe the car would try to hide in the shopping center or in the fairgrounds near there.

Still flying high above the ground, she sped in that direction. She marveled at the freedom she felt so high up in the air—she felt light as a feather.

She heard sirens again—a police car was also coming in the same direction as she was going.

Noelle flew back and forth above the parking lot several times. No sign of the blue car. She paused—amazed that she could hover there. The police car stopped at the entrance to the shopping center parking lot and the policeman on the passenger side was leaning out the window looking at her.

She glanced down at him, but then sped away from the shopping center and toward the fairgrounds. There it was! The blue car. It was partially hidden by some buildings, but she could clearly see the stick figures in the back window.

Having no idea what she would do when she reached the car, Noelle dived toward it. She glanced back, relieved to see the police car following her.

Noelle landed softly on the ground behind the blue car. There was no sign of Mollie or the driver. She sneaked around the car looking in the windows. One of Mollie's new dolls was on the floor in the back seat.

"Help! Someone, help me!"

Mollie's desperate cry came from inside the building and Noelle crept toward the door. She could hear the police car coming down the dirt road.

While trying to make up her mind if she should wait for the police—after all, what could a nine-year-old do against a kidnapper—a tall dark-haired man threw the door open and bolted from the building.

Noelle was so stunned, she froze. The man looked directly at her and then ran in the opposite direction and disappeared into some trees.

Noelle could hear Mollie crying, so she yelled to her, "Mollie it's okay. The police are here—I'll be right back!"

"Noelle!" yelled Mollie.

"It's okay, Mollie!" She hoped Mollie could hear her from inside the building.

Noelle jumped, and immediately she was air born. She flew above the trees and caught sight of the man running down the fence line of the fairgrounds. There was no gate in sight and the fence appeared too high for him to jump over. He stopped abruptly and began climbing the wood fence.

Noelle flew toward him and landed on top of the fence staring down at the man.

"Where are you going?" she said.

The startled man looked up, and when he saw Noelle, he fell backwards crashing to the ground on his back.

Noelle couldn't resist—she flew above him—hovering in the air.

"Who are you?" yelled the frightened man.

Noelle thought for a minute, and then she flew closer to him and stared into his eyes as he coward in the dirt.

"You shouldn't mess with my friend." She hissed.

"What the…?"

Noelle turned—two policeman and Mollie were running toward her.

The first policeman continued, "What—or who are you?"

Noelle softly landed on the ground next to the man. She ran to Mollie and threw her arms around her friend and both girls started crying.

The second policeman put the man on the ground in handcuffs and pulled him to his feet.

"She's a freak!" he yelled in Noelle's direction.

"Maybe, but she found you," said the first policeman. He turned to Noelle, "Now little girl—can you explain all of this?"

Noelle's eyes widened. "All of what?"

The policeman's eyes narrowed.

"Oh, you mean the flying thing. Yeah, I don't know. It just happened."

"You can fly?" Mollie stared at her friend.

"Yes, watch." Noelle shot into the air, zipped around in a circle above their heads and then quickly landed.

"Wow!" said Mollie.

"I know cool, huh?"

The policeman who had taken the man to the police car walked up to Mollie but watched Noelle from the corner of his eye. "Are you okay? Your parents are on their way to the police station. We have another patrol car on the way to pick you girls up and take you there."

Mollie looked at Noelle, "We could fly."

The second policeman chuckled nervously, "Uh no, that's okay. We'll take you in the car."

"I have to say that was pretty impressive," said the first policeman, "you lead us right to Mollie."

Noelle grinned as they walked past the blue car to the waiting patrol car. A policeman was holding the back door open for the two girls, but just as they reached it, Noelle turned around. She jumped in the air and flew back to the blue car—the back door was open, and she reached in to get Mollie's Monster High doll from the floor. That same old man from the playground was sitting on the back seat.

Startled, she stopped for a second, but then she grabbed the doll and quickly flew back to the patrol car. She looked over her shoulder as she flew. The old man was gone.

The man who had tried to kidnap Mollie was staring at Noelle from the back window of one police car.

All four policemen were also staring at her.

But Mollie's grin was so big it covered her whole face, and she took the doll from Noelle and hugged her friend.

Noelle turned to face the four policemen, "What? I had to go get her doll."

∽ 13 ∾

INVISIBLE RESCUE

"HURRY, BRIGHTON!"

Brighton said goodbye to her teammates and ran down the sidewalk to her mom's parked car. She pulled the back door open, threw her football bag and helmet on the seat and slammed the door shut. She pulled the front door open and climbed into the passenger seat.

"Geez, Mom, where's the fire?"

Mom gave her a side-glance as she steered the car slowly away from the curb. "No fire, but your dad needs us to pick him up at work. He didn't even make it back for your brother's practice today."

Brighton had noticed that her dad was not with her brother's team today, but then she moaned when she realized where they were going. "Oh, Mom, clear up there?"

"It's only a forty-five-minute drive Brighton. Your brother's practice doesn't end for another hour, so I had him ride home with Blake. Besides, I thought you wanted to go see Daddy work."

"I do…but I'm hungry."

"Taken care of." Mom motioned to a bag on the floor.

"Oh wow, cool. McDonalds!"

Mom laughed, "You were so busy whining you didn't even notice."

Brighton tore the bag open and pulled out a box of chicken nuggets. For other kids', fast food was a household name, but not at the Nessumsar house. This was an epic occasion for Brighton. Mom didn't believe in fast food, so Brighton and her brother hardly ever got it. Unless, of course, Dad could sneak it sometimes—and then there was her grandma—she took them to the fast-food giant whenever she was there, and funny thing, Mom never complained.

Brighton smiled, and after smothering a nugget in barbeque sauce she popped it into her mouth. "So, where's Dad's truck?"

"Don't talk with your mouth full, Brighton."

"Okay," Brighton said, still with a full mouth.

Mom rolled her eyes, "Apparently, one of the guys he works with had to leave early today because his wife went to the hospital to have her baby. She was supposed to pick her husband up from work, but the baby changed that plan."

"Oh, well when will he ever get his truck back?" Brighton took a long gulp of her sprite.

"Tomorrow, "Mom quickly followed up with, "and no you do not have to ride up again. I'll take Dad after you kids go to school."

"Well, I'll go if you buy me McDonalds again." Brighton grinned and licked the sauce from her lips.

Mom shook her head, "Uh no, that's okay. This is a once-a-year event."

Brighton sighed, knowing her mother was serious. She sank back into the seat to finish her treasured nuggets and French fries.

She jabbered all the way to Victorville, telling her mother all about her day at school and football practice. Usually, her mom was sitting on the sidelines at practice and knew everything that had happened, but today she had to drop her kids off so she could finish an appointment for work.

Brighton was the only girl player in the league, but she didn't care. She loved football. She had been watching her brother play since she was about four years old, and when she turned seven, she asked if she could play too. Mom and Dad were not too excited at first, and she knew they thought she would quit after one year. But she didn't. She loved it too much. She was fast too, but she always wished she could be faster. She hated the running drills her coach made them do. She knew if she tried harder at those, she probably would be faster. But sometimes, she just felt too lazy to run as hard as she could every single drill.

It didn't seem like forty-five minutes had passed when they pulled up to the site where Dad was working today. Mom confirmed it had taken nearly an hour.

Brighton concluded; the McDonalds treat had made the difference for her. Mom agreed, but Brighton knew it was just so she wouldn't talk non-stop about her nuggets, French fries, and sprite. Brighton also knew that when her brother found out he had missed the event, Mom would have to take him there soon, and secretly she hoped she could tag along when that day came.

Brighton climbed out of the car and followed her mother across a dirt path. She could see her dad perched high above the ground in a basket that was fastened to a huge, tall crane. Dad was sawing off the top of a power pole. He looked kind of small from way down here.

There was an old man in the basket with her dad.

"Who is that old man in dad's basket, Mom?"

"What old man?" Mom looked where Brighton pointed, "I don't see an old man, Brighton. The basket is only big enough for one person."

Brighton shrugged, now the old man was gone anyway.

One of the workers approached Brighton and Mom. "He's almost finished. It's going to be dark soon."

"Hi Rob. He said something about having to work a little longer since Trent had to leave."

Rob nodded and motioned to another crane and a group of men not far from where dad was. They were cutting down the tops of trees—*really* tall trees.

"I had those guys double up to get those trees down. We are supposed to get some rain tomorrow."

"Well, that will be a miracle," said Mom.

Rob sighed, "Yeah, seems like it only comes when we have this kind of work to get out of the way."

Brighton noticed that the pole her dad was working on and the trees the other men were working on all had ropes tied to them. She wondered what that was for. She was going to ask as soon as the man named Rob stopped talking. She was practicing not interrupting. She wasn't very good at it but right now she was distracted by a huge black crow that was sitting on top of a pole near her dad.

Rob continued, "What your dad is doing up there is very important."

Brighton turned her attention to Rob and nodded. "I know, he has told us a little bit about it."

Rob grinned, "I suppose he has. He must be very careful. See all those wires that are connected to the pole?"

Brighton nodded.

"Those are live wires; I mean they have electricity running through them. See the man at the bottom of the pole, watching your dad?"

Again, Brighton nodded.

Rob continued, "He is watching everything your dad does to make sure he doesn't make any mistakes."

"Will Dad get in trouble if he does?"

Rob sighed and exchanged a quick glance with Mom. "Yeah, something like that."

Brighton pointed to the crow that was still sitting on top of the pole. "Will that bird get hurt if he touches the wires?"

"That's a good question. Have you ever seen birds sitting on wires?"

"Yes, lots of times."

"Well, those birds do not get hurt because they are not grounded…"

"What?"

"He means, because they are only touching the wire, Brighton. If that crow touched the pole and the wire it would be electrocuted."

Mom shaded her eyes and looked up at the bird. "That is a pretty big crow. Does it come around here often?"

Rob shook his head, "Nope. At least I have never seen it."

"So could my dad get electrocuted?"

Rob nodded slowly, "He could, but do you see all the equipment up there? He is well protected. If he does not touch the wires he is just fine. Remember too, that your dad is really good at this and that man at the bottom is there to warn him, so not to worry."

Brighton nodded and instinctively took hold of her mom's hand.

She continued to look from her dad to the crow and back again. It seemed to her that the crow was looking right at her, and it made her feel a little strange. She looked at the men sawing down the trees. All the saws seemed to be going at once now and it was so loud Brighton covered her ears.

She watched as one of the saws cut clear through a treetop and it swung away from the men by the rope that was tied to it. Some men on the ground pulled on some other ropes and lowered the huge treetop to the ground.

The crow suddenly cawed and Brighton looked up just in time to see it dive from the top of the pole. She froze as the huge bird plunged directly at her.

"What the…?" yelled Rob.

"Brighton, look out!" Mom grabbed Brighton by the back of the head and shoved her to the ground and then fell next to her.

Brighton rolled to her back just in time to see the crow swoop just above her face and then immediately climb straight into the sky and disappear behind the trees. She could still hear its loud cawing when she could no longer see it.

Mom grabbed Brighton by the shoulders, "Did it hit you?"

"No, Mom." She put her hands over her ears again. The sound seemed to have intensified.

Mom started to stand, helping Brighton to her feet. "What kind of a freaky bird was that?"

Rob helped them both, all the while shaking his head. "Freaky is right. That was some huge bird."

Brighton looked up at her dad. He was just pulling his saw away from the pole and like the tree had done, the pole swung away from him by the ropes it was attached to.

Dad placed the chain saw on the floor of his basket and stood back up.

It was at that second that Brighton heard a loud snap and saw a rope pull away from one of the trees the men were sawing.

The man on the ground was yelling at Dad, Rob ran toward the man, and he too was yelling at her dad.

The men who were cutting the trees ducked inside their baskets and one of the chain saws fell toward the ground.

Brighton could see what was about to happen. The huge treetop was heading right for her dad.

Suddenly, as though something had shocked her, Brighton's entire body tingled, and she started running toward the huge crane that held her dad's basket.

"Brighton!" screamed Mom.

But Brighton did not stop. She was not sure why, but she kept running. As she got closer to the crane she leaped, and to her surprise she soared straight up into the sky right toward her dad. Shocked by her new ability she seemed to know exactly what to do. She changed her direction and in a split second was facing the oncoming treetop.

She grabbed the rope that was still attached to the tree and pulled with all her strength until it swung in the opposite direction away from her dad. As she did, she noticed her dad's basket lowering, but now the tree was headed back toward the men who had chopped it down.

She whirled, and seeming to run in the air, again she was in front of the tree. This time with both feet, she shoved the huge trunk away from the men. Now their basket too was lowering. The treetop swung back toward them again, but it was too high to hit them, and it was left to swing back and forth, still hanging from one of the two ropes that had held it in place.

Curious now, Brighton turned in the direction the massive crow had gone. She was immediately over the treetops and out of sight of the workers and her parents. The crow was nowhere to be found, but there was that old man again. The one from the basket, with the white hair.

Suddenly, she heard a loud caw and looked up in time to see the bird diminish into a tiny dot and disappear into the cloudy sky.

Brighton turned and ran back through the air to where her parents were. The tree was still swinging dangerously back and forth and the men on the ground were moving equipment out of its path.

Brighton lowered herself to the ground and ran toward her dad who, along with Rob, was hurrying away from the path of the swinging tree.

"Brighton!" Mom was screaming at her daughter.

"I'm here, Mom!" Brighton made sure she landed on the ground behind her mother.

Mom whirled around, "But, I thought I saw you run toward your dad?"

Brighton hurried to her mother's side. "No, Mom, why would I do that? I…I started to, but then I turned around. I didn't want to get hit by the tree."

Mom threw her arms around Brighton and pulled her close. "You scared me to death. For a minute I thought I would lose you and your dad."

"I'm okay, Mom, really."

Rob was walking toward them now. "That was a miracle," he mumbled, as he walked by them and climbed into the cab of a truck. He picked up a phone and said something into it. She heard him say her dad's name.

Brighton heard sirens in the distance and in minutes they were screaming toward them.

Two police cars, an ambulance and a fire truck all pulled to a stop near the cranes, and the policemen, fire fighters and paramedics jumped out.

Mom pulled Brighton back away from the commotion. "Let's

go get in the car, Brighton. Daddy will be here in a few minutes. He's, he's okay."

Brighton realized her mom was crying and she hugged her arm. "Its' okay, Mom. Everyone will be okay."

"I... I know, I just don't know how that could be possible. That tree was heading right for your dad. It's like something literally pushed it away from him."

"Well, maybe it did." Brighton's eyes lit up and her mom looked down at her. Tears were still streaming down her face. She hugged her daughter again. "But...? Oh, maybe it did. I just don't see how that was possible."

"I don't know, Mom."

The two reached the car now and Mom unlocked the door for Brighton, and she climbed into the back seat. Mom didn't get in, she just leaned against the car and Brighton knew she was still crying.

Brighton stared into the sky, her mind racing. The big bird had nearly hit her. When she stood up, the sound of the saws seemed louder. The bird's cawing was especially loud. Her entire body tingled like electricity, and when she ran and jumped, she flew into the sky. She was not sure how, but she had managed to grab the rope and pull the tree away from her dad and then push it away from the other men.

Brighton looked at her hands. They were red from grabbing the rope, and the tingling sensation in her hands feel like when she slept on them wrong. She slumped against the seat.

What had just happened to her? Should she tell mom and dad? Should she tell her brother? Her best friend, Nadia?

"Brighton?"

Brighton looked up at the sound of Dad's voice.

"You okay, honey?"

Brighton climbed out of the car and was immediately sandwiched in a tight hug between her parents.

Brighton nodded, but neither of her parents seemed to notice. Mom was crying again.

Dad looked down at his daughter, "Sorry about that scare, Brighton. Are you sure you're, okay?"

"I am, Dad, really. I'm perfectly fine."

I think. And she realized that she could not only fly and become invisible, but she was super strong too. She looked up into the sky.

Where did that crow go? And that old guy?

∽ 14 ∾

REAL DOLLS ARE MORE FUN

AVA CAREFULLY POSITIONED her American Girl Doll on her own little beach towel. She propped her head up on another towel so she could see Ava and Trixie while they played in the ocean.

"Wouldn't it be cool if our American Girl Dolls were real people?"

Trixie laughed, "Yeah, but then they wouldn't have to do what we tell them to do."

"Well, I mean that would be part of it. They would be real—but still be dolls."

Trixie scrunched her face. "That's silly. They would have to eat."

"No—they would be dolls—they wouldn't have to eat. They could just play with us and then we could put them back and they would be quiet." Ava threw her arms in the air and spun in a circle. "That would be just too cool."

Trixie giggled, "You're crazy. But that *would* be cool."

The girls ran away from a huge wave that was breaking just offshore, but they were too late, and it drenched them both.

They came out of the water laughing and sputtering.

"And they couldn't drown either," yelled Ava.

They trudged through the sand to their towels—their respective American Girl Dolls still in the same positions they had left them.

Both girls collapsed on the sand.

"Hey Ava—Mom wants you to come in now!" Ava's older brother came just close enough for her to hear him and then spun around and jogged back across the sand.

The girls sighed, gathered their dolls, towels, and flip flops, and followed Ava's brother.

When they reached the boardwalk a short horn blast caught their attention.

"Trixie over here." Trixie's mother stood next to her car with the door open.

"Coming Mom. See you at school tomorrow, Ava." and Trixie ran ahead.

Ava slowed down a little bit. She crossed the boardwalk in front of an old man who curiously stopped, waiting for her to cross. Ava looked at him, but then went on her way. She glanced over her shoulder; he was gone. She looked down the boardwalk. He wasn't there either.

Ava dismissed the old man and looked into her doll's clear blue eyes. "I think it would be cool if you could come to life and play with me, Zarina. Then after dinner we could read." Ava smiled at Zarina, and the doll's pretty expression smiled right back.

"Are you seriously talking to your doll again?"

"Shut up." Ava whirled around when she heard her younger brother.

"Ava has lost it—Ava has lost it!" He teased and ran away when she tossed one of her flip flops at him.

He disappeared through the back door and Ava again turned to Zarina. "Don't mind him. He's a dork."

She smoothed Zarina's long blonde hair and imagined how fun it would be to have her as a playmate when her real girlfriends had to go home.

Ava sighed, giggled as she hugged her treasured doll and turned to go in the house. When she reached for the doorknob, a loud cawing sound scared her, and she dropped her other flip flop. Struggling to keep Zarina in her arms, she tripped and landed on her knees.

The shrill cawing got even louder, and she crouched down on the cement.

Ava lifted her head and peeked to see what was making the sound, but just when she did, a huge black bird flew directly at her, nearly hitting her in the back of the head.

Ava scrambled to her feet and ran into the garage slamming the door behind her.

Still clutching her doll, Ava pressed her nose against the glass in the door trying to see the bird, but it was long gone.

Her heart was pounding so hard she could barely breathe when she hurried inside the house.

"What's wrong with you?" asked Mom when Ava bound into the kitchen.

"Noth…nothing, except this huge bird scared me to death."

"A Pelican?" said Mom.

"Nope it was black—and it made a sound like this, caw—caw…"

"Humph—why did it scare you?"

"It flew right at me! I think it was trying to attack me!"

Mom chuckled, "I doubt that Ava, but I'm glad you're okay."

"Me too! We could have been killed."

"Killed? By a bird?" Ava's older brother trotted down the stairs, "and besides, your doll couldn't be killed, she's not alive!"

"That's enough." Mom warned. "Ava, hurry and go shower—dinner is almost ready."

Ava glared at her brother and just before her foot hit the bottom step, she glanced at mom to see if she was looking. When she clearly wasn't, Ava stuck her tongue out at her brother, but he wasn't looking either.

Safe inside her bedroom, Ava placed her doll on her bed. "I really do wish you could be alive. We could play after dinner."

Her doll's happy smile and twinkling eyes stared back at Ava.

"Oh well," said Ava, and she hurried into the shower.

Ava felt kind of funny while she showered—kind of tingly and especially happy.

She turned the water off and stepped out of the shower, grabbed a towel, and wrapped it around her.

"Is it my turn?"

Ava froze. "Who said that?"

"Me—I'm out here."

Ava crept slowly to the bathroom door and cracked it open. She peered through the opening. "Is that you, Mom?" She knew the voice was a girl and Mom was the only other girl in the house.

"No silly, it's me."

Her heart pounding even harder than when she had seen the bird, Ava quickly closed the door staring at her blank expression in the foggy mirror.

"Don't be afraid, Ava. I thought you wanted me to come and play with you."

Ava was shaking now and not because she was cold. She grabbed her nightgown, pulled it over her head, and then taking a deep breath, she slowly opened the door again.

"Hi!"

Ava screamed and jumped back into the bathroom, but she didn't close the door.

There sitting on her bed was her American Girl Doll—only she was a full-sized girl. And she was—she was…talking!

"What the…?"

"You wished for me to be alive," her doll grinned.

"Yeah but—but…"

"You didn't think it would happen, did you?"

"No—no…" stammered Ava.

Zarina jumped to her feet. "Well, here I am."

Ava was speechless.

"What do you want to do? Are we going to read a story?"

Ava felt her mouth hanging open as she continued to stare at her doll—only not really a doll—a—a doll person.

"Look, this is how it works," said Zarina. "Think of me being a doll."

Ava shrugged.

"But" Zarina quickly added, "then immediately think of me being alive."

Ava's eyes narrowed, "What?"

"Just do it."

Ava couldn't believe she was taking orders from her doll. She took a deep breath and let it slowly escape her lips. She twisted her mouth and closed her eyes, thinking of her American Girl Doll sitting on the bed—just being a doll.

Ava gasped when she opened her eyes. There was her doll! Just like she had left her when she went into the shower.

"Whew," breathed Ava, but she stood still for several minutes.

I think I may be crazy.

Suddenly, she remembered. *'Then immediately think of me being alive.'*

Ava closed her eyes, but then she opened them just a tiny bit so that she could kind of see Zarina.

She thought of the doll being alive again.

"Hi! See, I told you."

Ava's eyes widened. "Wow."

"All you have to do is think of me being alive and I'll be here to play with you. Cool huh?"

"So totally cool," squealed Ava.

"Ava!"

"Coming, Mom!" she grinned at Zarina, "wait till I tell Mom!"

"No. You can't tell anyone. This is our secret."

Ava had to think about that for a minute, then she said, "Can I make other things appear?"

"Probably, try it."

Ava squinted her eyes and thought of a little dog.

"Ruff! Ruff!"

Ava jumped back, and the little brown dog kept barking.

She quickly thought of the dog gone and it immediately disappeared.

"Wow!" Ava shrieked.

"Before you go to dinner you need to think of me as a doll."

Ava giggled. She ran toward the door, but then turned around. "As soon as you're a doll again, I am going to think of something for my mom."

"What?" said Zarina, just before she returned to being a doll.

"A corvette!" Ava ran down the stairs, right past the kitchen and pulled open the front door. Their house faced a busy street on the peninsula, so different cars parked in the space in front of their house.

"It worked!"

"Ava, what are you doing? What worked?"

"Come and see, Mom."

Ava's brothers and her mother joined her at the open door. Ava pointed to the shiny white corvette parked right in front of their house.

Seemingly annoyed, her older brother asked, "What are we looking at?" He was in middle school and thought everything was dumb.

"That corvette. I imagined it and it's here."

Her brother rolled his eyes, "Ava lots of people park on this street. You did not imagine it."

Ava glared at him, "Yes I did, watch."

Ava closed her eyes and imagined the corvette was gone, but when she opened her eyes, it was still there.

Her little brother laughed, "You've really lost it, Ava."

Mom said, "It's okay, Ava, maybe next time. Come on, breakfast is ready, and you have to leave for school soon."

Ava's brothers followed their mom, but Ava still stood at the open door. Her eyebrows furrowed, *why couldn't I make it go away?*

She closed her eyes again and imagined the corvette gone. This time when she opened them, the corvette really was gone.

Ava ran to the kitchen, "Come here, the car is gone!"

Curiously, her little brother followed Ava back to the front door. "It is gone!" he called to whoever was listening.

Ava felt so proud that she had accomplished making the corvette disappear, but her older brother laughed when she joined them back in the kitchen, "Of course it's gone, someone drove it away."

Mom and her brothers laughed.

"It's okay, Ava, it's fun to pretend," said Mom.

"But" Ava protested, but then she decided not to say anymore. Puzzled, she ate her dinner in silence.

Ava trudged up to her room to get her backpack. As she approached her bedroom door, she imagined Zarina alive again. She hesitated outside the door, but then slowly she opened it.

There was Zarina, a real live girl sitting on her bed.

Ava grinned, "Hi! So, it didn't work with the corvette. I mean it did, but when I tried to make it disappear I couldn't, but then I could."

"You left so fast I didn't get to tell you that you can't do this in front of people. Others can see what you make appear and disappear, but not *while* you do it."

Ava sat on her bed, "Oh." Then she asked, "Why can I do this anyway?"

Zarina shrugged just like a real girl would, "I don't know. Has anything strange happened to you lately?"

Ava shook her head, "Not really..." she put her elbows on her knees and stared at the floor.

Zarina pushed lightly on Ava's shoulder, "Think, there must be something."

Suddenly Ava sat up, "There was this bird."

Zarina looked surprised, "A bird?"

"Yes, a great big black bird. It was so weird. When I was coming in from the beach, I was carrying you, and this huge bird flew at me. It almost hit me and then it flew away."

Zarina didn't look convinced, "So, you think the bird gave you this power?"

Now Ava shrugged, "I don't know, it's the only thing I can think of that has been different than normal." She looked at Zarina, "how do you know that it only works when people are not looking?"

Zarina's eyes widened, "I'm not sure. I don't have much experience being alive. I just knew to tell you that."

Ava sighed, "This is just too weird, and my family, well my brothers, think I'm crazy."

"Of course, they do. You're a girl." Zarina laughed.

The next morning Ava got ready for school all the time chatting with Zarina.

Ava threw her backpack over her shoulder, "Guess I better imagine you're a doll again?"

Zarina giggled, "Yes, but even if you didn't, your mom wouldn't see me as a girl if she came in here while you were gone."

"How do you know?"

Zarina thought for a minute, "I'm not sure. I just know." She stood and walked over to the American Girl Doll bed that was made especially for her. She yawned, "Besides I don't have anything to do if you're gone, and if I have to stay in this room all day, I would rather sleep."

"So, you sleep when you're a doll?"

"I don't know what I do, but I know I don't want to be a girl if you're not here. How fun is that?"

Ava laughed.

"Ava, it's time to leave!" called her mother from the hallway.

Ava closed her eyes, but then she quickly opened them again, "Bye, see you later."

Zarina waved, "Bye."

Ava closed her eyes and imagined Zarina a doll again. When she opened her eyes her American Girl doll was positioned perfectly on her special bed.

Ava stood quietly for a minute marveling at this new talent she had. She was sad she couldn't share it with anyone.

"Ava!"

"Coming, Mom."

Ava hurried out the door and down the hall. She would have to think about this later, right now she had to go to school.

She and her little brother kissed their mom good-bye, got on their bikes, and headed off to the boardwalk to ride the few blocks to school. Her older brother had already left, since he was in middle school and went a different direction.

Ava rode alongside her little brother who chattered non-stop. After several minutes of Ava's silence, he said, "It would be cool if you could make stuff appear, Ava."

Surprised by his comment, Ava grinned, "Yeah it would be."

"If you do figure it out, could you make a new soccer ball appear for me? Mom said I have to wait till my birthday for one and that's months away."

Ava stared at her little brother for as long as she dared while riding her bike, "Are you serious?"

Her little brother laughed, suddenly looking embarrassed, "No, just kidding."

But somehow Ava knew he wasn't kidding.

The day seemed to drag more slowly than usual. Ava wanted to tell Trixie about her new talent, but she didn't dare. She decided she should wait till later when they were alone. She contemplated all day how she would tell her so Trixie would believe her.

Finally, the bell rang, and Ava hurried out the door to her bike. Her little brother was staying for an arts and crafts class, so Ava rode home alone. She had thought of an idea and wanted to see if it would work. Her brothers would be home in less than an hour, so she had to work fast.

As she rode down the boardwalk, she saw the same old man from yesterday.

Maybe he just moved here.

He seemed strange to Ava, but she dismissed him again and concentrated on her plan.

"Hi, Mom!"

"I'm upstairs, Ava."

"Okay," and she ran to her room to check on Zarina. She was still on the little bed right where Ava had left her before she left for school.

Ava hurried downstairs and out to the front porch. She closed her eyes and imagined a new soccer ball. When she opened her eyes, it was there on the cement, right in front of her.

Ava squealed. She couldn't wait for her brothers to get home.

Suddenly she thought, "Wait, what if they can't even see it, or what if they can and then it disappears after a while?"

Ava thought for several minutes about this problem. She couldn't imagine that anything she thought of could appear and then stay there. Think of all the things she could have.

No, there must be rules. She would figure them out. But in the meantime, she hoped the soccer ball would be real, and that her brother could keep it.

When her brother came in from the garage, Ava made sure she was sitting at the kitchen table having a snack. He went straight to the fridge and pulled out a carton of orange juice, poured a glass and went into the living room. Ava could see he had no intention of going out to the front porch.

Suddenly, she had an idea. She imagined the doorbell ringing, but so she would be certain her brother answered it, she quickly started upstairs.

"Ava, aren't you going to answer the door?"

"I'm halfway upstairs, you get it."

She heard him grumble when he passed the stairs and she giggled. She stopped at the top of the stairs and waited.

"What the?"

She heard the door slam and her brother call, "Someone left a new soccer ball!"

Ava could hear him ripping the box apart, and at the same time, Mom and her older brother came in from the garage.

Mom asked, "Where did you get that soccer ball?"

"It was on the porch, right in front of the..." her brother stopped talking for a minute and then he called, "Ava!"

Ava ducked inside her bedroom and quietly closed the door. She giggled again and then imagined her American Doll being alive.

This is going to be fun.

∽ 15 ∾

JOG-A-THONS ARE DUMB

ZION MOANED, "Do we have to do the Jog-a-thon again?"

Miss Miller smiled, "Yes Zion, everyone has to participate. C'mon it will be fun."

"It isn't fun," moaned Zion again. "I always lose."

"Well maybe you won't lose this year! This is your year to win." Miss Miller sounded way too enthusiastic for Zion. In the second grade now, this would be the third time he had run in the jog-a-thon. He didn't win in kindergarten, or first grade, and he didn't expect to win this time either. It wasn't that he couldn't run fast. It was just that he got tired and didn't *want* to run fast.

Zion began having flashbacks of the jog-a-thon races in kindergarten and first grade. He liked to run, but he didn't like the pressure of competition and being forced to run fast. In Kindergarten he started out great, but then he slowed down in the middle of that race. At that time the course was in a big circle and the students ran around as many times as they could. They got credit for each completed course, and the winner got a trophy. But Zion got bored running around and around and around.

That year his sister won the trophy from her grade.

When his brother was in kindergarten, he won the trophy for his grade, and he won it again in third grade. He would probably win again this year too.

135

Zion scowled.

This race is stupid. Why can't we go give the homeless people money and food? That's what mom does. But no, we have a dumb race.

He felt someone looking at him and he turned to see Susie McDonald smiling. She was staring at him! His eyes widened when he noticed an old man with white hair stood right behind Susie.

He started to say something, but then the old man disappeared.

Zion hurriedly looked away and sank down in his chair. *What is she so happy about? Maybe she is thinking that she will beat me. No, Susie is nice. She's probably thinking how fun this will be, but this is her first year at our school, so she doesn't know. Boy, is she in for a surprise?*

Zion closed his eyes and tried to imagine what it would be like to cross the finish line first. Would the tape break? Or would it catch him and fling him backwards?

No, the tape couldn't be that hard to break. After all, Jenna Wellington broke it in first grade and she's a girl.

Then he thought of the cheering from the crowd if he won. Would there be lots of cheering? What if someone booed him? What if he fell just as he crossed the finish line?

He groaned, *what if I fall…*he paused, *who am I kidding? I'm not going to win anyway.*

He felt a hand on his shoulder, and he realized Miss Miller was talking to the whole class, "This activity is for a good cause. We help a lot of homeless people with the money you raise from your pledges for the laps you run."

That's what Miss Miller did when she could see someone was not paying attention. She put her hand on their shoulder, and Zion was not paying attention.

He scowled but quickly changed expression when his mom stepped through the door of their classroom. She was here to volunteer.

Maybe he could pretend to be sick—or maybe say his leg hurt—no, maybe his head.

Mom walked right over to Zion. She smiled and ruffled his hair.

"Ready?"

Zion quickly glanced at Susie McDonald. Did she see Mom ruffle his hair?

She was looking away.

He breathed a sigh of relief and looked at the floor, "Yeah," he mumbled.

"What's the matter?" Mom knelt beside him.

"Mom it's terrible. I never win. I wish I could run faster than lightening."

He knew what his mom was going to say. That he could if he wanted to—and that his older brother and sister had to learn to run fast too.

He had no sooner thought all of that when his mom said, "Remember your brother and sister had to learn to run fast too."

"Yeah, but they always win."

"You can too." Mom ruffled his hair again as she stood. "You'll be awesome!"

Zion rolled his eyes and looked from the corner of his eye at Susie McDonald again. This time she saw, and she giggled.

Mom went outside to get her volunteer assignment and Zion went back to moping.

To make things even worse, the jog-a-thon would not be a circle of laps this year—instead, straight down the beach and back. They were supposed to run that course as many times as they could, because each lap down and each lap back counts toward their dollars they can earn. There was also that big trophy for the winner in each grade, but Zion had no hopes of winning that. Although, it would be nice to have one to put next to his sister and brothers on the fireplace mantle.

He trudged outside with the rest of his class where they met in a huge circle that had been drawn on the sand.

The waves crashed against the shore only a few yards from the playground, and Zion wished it was after school and he was playing with his boogie board.

The principal was explaining the course to the students, how it was down and back and the winner in each class would be the one who did the most laps—and that student would be the one who broke the tape because they would be that last one running.

"Usually," added the principal, "but we'll call out the laps to make sure we have the right winner. After all, some kids run faster than others."

Zion rolled his eyes. *You got that right.*

He stood on his tiptoes to see the course. *It looks like a million miles!*

But then he saw Susie McDonald smiling again and he forced a smile back.

Zion looked across the sea of white T-shirts and blue shorts. Every single kid in school was dressed the same.

Maybe I can disappear.

The kindergarten and first grade had completed their races, now it was the second graders turn. The students were led to the starting line, given some brief instructions, the whistle blew, and the first group of runners took off. The rest of the students and the parents cheered them on.

Finally, it was time for Zion's class, and he stepped up to the line…the whistle blew, and he sprinted ahead of everyone. For a few seconds he felt like he had a chance but was quickly overtaken by nearly everyone in his class. He sighed and slowed to a jog.

What's the use?

Zion reached the first turn around point and started back with some of the other kids who had slowed down like him.

He was distracted by a dog barking. He looked in the direction of the sound and saw a little yellow dog struggling to get out of the water as the waves kept crashing over him.

Zion looked around but no one else seemed to notice. He knew if he left the race to help the dog, he would lose for sure, but the little dog looked helpless, and Zion knew if he didn't help, it would drown.

He looked around again to see if an adult was close by, but they were all watching the race, and he knew he wouldn't be heard over the cheering parents even if he yelled his loudest.

Suddenly Zion turned and ran off the track and into the water. As he got closer, he could see the dog was caught in some seaweed, but when he reached the dog, he realized seaweed wasn't the problem. The little dog's legs were tangled in fishing line.

Zion lifted the dog out of the water and held it while he untangled its legs from the line. He walked up the beach a little and put the dog on the sand. He rubbed its legs where there were little cuts from the sharp line.

The dog kept trying to lick Zion's face, making him laugh.

"Cocoa!"

Zion looked up to see a lady running in their direction.

"How did you get out?" said the lady.

The little dog broke free from Zion and ran to the lady who scooped it up in her arms and hugged it to her chest. She waved to Zion, but she didn't say anything.

Zion shrugged, of course the lady didn't know he saved her dog from certain death.

He scoffed and turned his attention back to the race knowing full well they would be on their second or third lap by now. He was shocked to see the kids who had been in front of him seemed to be just a few feet from where they were when he left the course.

Encouraged, but not knowing how that happened, he brushed the sand from his knees and hands and started to run, but just as he did, he felt something nearly hit his head, and at the same time, a loud cawing sound. He looked up to see a huge crow right above him. He could feel the wind from its wings, and he dived to the sand covering his head.

"Help!" he yelled, but his cry fell on deaf ears.

The crow came at him again brushing the back of his head with its wings and Zion's eyes filled with tears.

"Help!" he cried again.

He lay perfectly still, realizing the crow must be gone, because now the air was completely silent. He couldn't even hear the noise from the race.

Zion lifted his head. Everything seemed to be stopped. He looked around him; the waves were silent, the race was silent, even the air wasn't moving.

Zion stood again. As he did, he felt a surge of energy go through him and he bolted forward, now determined to catch his friends.

When he reached the running course, the same old man he had seen earlier was there. Zion slowed a little, but the man disappeared.

Zion shook his head.

Wow. I need to tell Mom about that guy.

He could hear the ocean now, the noise from the race, and his own heart beating. He was excited and he ran harder.

Zion could feel his legs were moving faster and faster—he looked down, his legs were a blur. He was running so fast, he soon caught up with all the other kids, and in seconds he whizzed right past all of them with only two runners ahead of him. He was running so fast he couldn't feel his feet touching the ground.

The crowd was screaming his name and he heard his brother above them all, "Zion, you can win! You can win!"

Zion hit the starting line, making sure he touched the line with his foot, then spun around with just a couple of kids ahead of him and a few close behind.

He could hear his sister screaming his name too, and his heart soared. He was still a few feet behind the two lead runners. The boy pulled a little ahead of the girl, but then she surged forward, catching him again.

Soon he passed the two lead runners and he turned again at the appointed spot. He ran and he ran, and he ran.

Everything was a blur. He kept running and running until he heard the principal's voice.

"Zion! You can break the tape. You are the last runner on the course."

Zion glanced around. He was running alone.

This was it—the finish line was only a few feet away.

Zion took a huge deep breath, put his head down and charged forward as hard as he could. He burst through the tape and felt it only slightly on his chest but saw the two ends flitter to the ground in front of him.

The screaming of the crowd was deafening, but he could hear his family above them all.

His friends crowded around him, and his brother and a friend lifted him upon their shoulders. Zion was grinning so big he was sure his cheeks might crack.

He saw his mom, "I did it! I did it!"

Dad patted him on the back. Mom gave him a huge squeeze. She laughed and embarrassed him when she kissed his cheek.

His sister squealed, "Zion that was awesome! You ran like a hundred laps."

Zion shrugged and then he caught Susie McDonald's eye. She was grinning from ear to ear and Zion grinned right back.

He saw Miss Miller walking in his direction, her face beaming. The principal was right behind her with a microphone in his hand. Miss Miller walked right up to Zion and gave him a hug. The principal gave him a high five.

"That was incredible, Zion. I told you this was your year to win," said Miss Miller.

Zion turned to his mom and yelled, "Did you see me, Mom? I ran faster than lightening!"

PRINCESSES CAN DO WHATEVER THEY WANT

"Now you sit right here, I'll be back in a minute." Micah scooted around the three cats and hurried to the kitchen. She returned seconds later with three saucers of milk—something she knew she wasn't supposed to do—but well, the cats liked milk.

She knew her mother didn't care how much the cats liked milk—but Micah did—so she hurried and gave it to them before Mom got home from work. Then she quickly washed the saucers and put them away.

No one will ever know.

She picked up her Hello Kitty purse and put on her Hello Kitty jacket and her Hello Kitty shoes and then she went into the back yard to play with her dolls and her Hello Kitty lunchbox, the three cats following close behind.

"What are you doing now?" Her older brother leaned over the railing on the patio deck.

"I'm playing," said Micah.

"It will be amazing if you don't turn into a cat someday," he snickered.

Micah didn't say anything to her brother, but when he turned around to go back in the house, she pulled a face.

Maybe I will!

Being the youngest of five children, she always felt like she was picked on. She didn't know why she had to do jobs that seemed too big for her. Unloading the silverware from the dishwasher or sweeping the floor.

Her mom and dad assured her that she wasn't being picked on, that she was expected to help around the house—especially when her parents weren't home. But Micah thought differently.

She was positive she was a princess. What princess had to do such menial tasks? She wasn't Cinderella after all, she didn't wear rags or get treated mean by her mom or siblings. She was a princess, and princesses are supposed to have maids and helpers and stuff. Where were her maids and helpers? She sighed and picked up the black kitten and stroked its fur.

Her favorite thing was to pretend that she was a *beautiful* princess who was a prisoner in a castle and her three cats would rescue her—then she would happily join them and become a kitty—a princess kitty of course.

But then everyone teased her and called her Hello Kitty Princess, and she would get mad and go to her room. But really, she liked that they called her that. Then she could pretend that they were the mean people who locked her up—even though she went to her room all on her own.

Soon, Mom came home, and it was time for dinner. Micah took the cats back in the house and they went to sleep on their three-story cat perch. She noticed a man on the sidewalk outside as she peered out the window. He had white hair and was very old. Micah shuddered and closed the blinds.

After dinner, Micah helped mom load the dishwasher. She made sure she loaded the three saucers she had put milk in for the cats. Even though she had washed them once, she wanted to wash them again, just in case.

Micah got ready for bed. Tomorrow was Saturday and they were all going to the pool to swim and have lunch. Micah loved to swim so she couldn't wait.

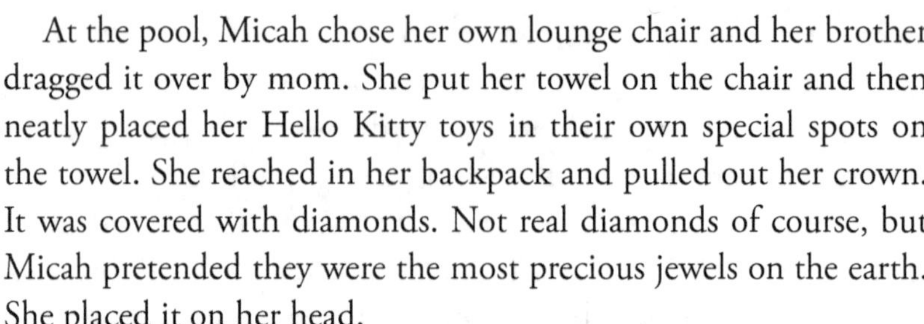

At the pool, Micah chose her own lounge chair and her brother dragged it over by mom. She put her towel on the chair and then neatly placed her Hello Kitty toys in their own special spots on the towel. She reached in her backpack and pulled out her crown. It was covered with diamonds. Not real diamonds of course, but Micah pretended they were the most precious jewels on the earth. She placed it on her head.

"Aren't you going to swim, Micah?" asked Mom.

"Yep, in a minute. First I need to get everything arranged."

"Arranged?" Dad walked up behind her and sat down next to mom.

"Yep, so they will be safe and sound while I swim."

"What are you going to do with your crown?"

Micah looked at her mother and pulled a face. "I will leave it here for Hello Kitty to protect."

"Ohhh." Mom smiled.

It wasn't long before Micah was splashing around in the water with her sister and brother. They slid down the slides and played in the waterfall. They climbed on the obstacle course and jumped into the water from the side. They did that so many times that Micah felt waterlogged when Mom called them for lunch.

They all sat down on the lounge chairs and ate pizza, breadsticks, and cinnamon churros. The churros were Micah's favorite, but she couldn't have one until she ate her pizza.

While they were eating, Micah noticed a big black bird sitting on the sidewalk.

She stared at it for a while, then she said to her mother, "Look at that bird."

"Good grief that is a big bird," said Mom.

"I think that's the biggest crow I've ever seen," said Dad. He walked over to the fence. "I wonder what it's doing?"

The bird was on the other side of the fence, and it didn't even move when dad approached.

"It's glaring at Dad," said her brother.

"Oh, it's not glaring. Birds don't glare," said Mom.

But dad had a funny look on his face when he turned around. "No, I actually think it's glaring."

Mom laughed, "Oh brother."

Dad raised his eyebrows, "Think what you want. I'd say that bird is glaring," and he winked at Micah.

After lunch was cleaned up everyone went back to the pool, but Micah stayed to play with her Hello Kitty toys.

She noticed a girl and her mother walking across the parking lot. The girl had on a Hello Kitty swimsuit and was carrying a Hello Kitty towel.

That same old man she had seen in her front yard was standing next to a car.

Micah jumped up and ran to the fence. She watched as the girl and her mother passed by—the girl smiled, and Micah smiled back. She looked at the old man again. He was gone.

Suddenly, the girl's mother screamed, "Little girl, watch out!"

Micah turned around just in time to see that same big black bird flying right at her. She screamed and covered her face with her hands.

"Micah!" Her older brother must have seen the bird and he ran toward his sister. He scooped her up in his arms and pulled her away from the fence.

"What happened?" Dad was running toward them.

"That bird—the one that you saw—it nearly hit Micah," said her brother.

The lady who yelled at Micah was standing by the fence. "It seemed like it was deliberately flying right at her," said the lady.

Her brother nodded, "It really did, Dad. I saw it from the pool."

"Are you okay?" Dad took Micah from her brother's arms.

Micah nodded. "It didn't hit me, but it scared me."

"Let's go sit down for a minute," said Mom.

When Micah was on her lounge chair, she looked back to where she had been when the bird flew at her. Something strange had happened then. When the bird flew at her, its wing hit her head. It didn't hurt, but it felt like a tiny pin poked her. Since then, she felt a tingling sensation all the way through her body, but she didn't tell Mom or Dad.

When they got home, Mom told Micah to take a bath and get into her pajamas. Then her mother checked her all over to make sure the bird hadn't scratched her.

"She seems fine," said Mom when she and Dad tucked Micah into bed.

The house was quiet when Micah woke up in the morning and she wondered where everybody was. She jumped out of bed and ran into the bathroom, but she stopped when she saw her reflection in the mirror. She clapped her hands over her mouth and looked at the girl in the mirror.

She wasn't just a girl, she was a princess, wearing a long, beautiful dress.

Micah closed her eyes and twirled around as her princess gown swooshed around her ankles.

I'm a princess! I'm princess! And she twirled some more.

Suddenly she stopped. "What is that?" she said out loud.

Micah turned slowly to look behind her. Sure enough—a big bushy cat tail poked out from under her beautiful princess skirt.

She swayed back and forth, and the tail swayed too.

"WOW! I have a tail!"

Micah jumped up and down! "Yay! I'm a kitty! I'm a kitty!"

Something dropped from the counter, and she picked it up. It was a wand—with a Hello Kitty top.

Micah twirled the wand and suddenly she was a kitty—no princess gown—just a beautiful white kitty.

She jumped up on the counter so she could see herself better. For a minute she looked back down at the floor, surprised at how easily she had gotten up on the counter.

She shrugged and turned back to the mirror. "I am beautiful!"

She rubbed her cheek against her shoulder and made a soft purring sound.

Suddenly, she had a thought. She jumped off the counter and picked the wand up with her paws. She twirled it around and sure enough—she was a princess again!

"This is so cool. Wait till I tell Mom and Dad!"

As she stepped out of the bathroom, there were her three kittens. They were standing curiously on their back legs, and each had a folded towel in its paws.

Micah giggled, "Are you my three helpers?"

The cats mewed, and Micah's eyes widened when they all three bowed before her.

This is so unbelievable! I am a princess—and a kitty—and my kittens are my helpers, just like I wished.

Micah looked one more time at her wonderful bushy tail—her beautiful pink princess gown and the glistening crown that was now perched on her head. She opened the bathroom door and called, "Hey you guys! Remember when you said I might someday turn into a cat?"

"Yeah so?" called her brother from the backyard, and Micah ran to the door where she could see her entire family through the window. She threw open the door and jumped onto the patio.

"Ta da! I'm a Hello Kitty Princess, just like you said!"

No one said a word—they just stared at her.

Then her brother said, "Actually, you're a princess, well, in a princess dress."

Micah held her Hello Kitty wand and lifted her pink princess skirt. With her tail swishing behind her, she pranced down the steps—like any princess kitty would do.

When she reached the bottom of the steps, she stopped and grinned. She realized they had not seen her tail.

Her family stared at her saying nothing.

Finally, Mom said, "What, Micah?"

Micah couldn't quit grinning, "Watch."

She spun her wand and instantly she was a beautiful white kitty.

Everyone gasped and Micah laughed. She hurriedly spun the wand again and returned to being a princess.

"You—you still have a tail," said her sister.

Micah swished her tail back and forth, "I know, isn't it cool?"

"Can you get back to being a girl—just a regular girl?" asked Mom quietly.

Micah thought she saw tears in her mom's eyes. She shrugged, "Geez, Mom, don't cry."

"It's a little strange, Micah," said dad.

Micah sighed. She looked curiously at her wand and then placed it on the grass. Instantly, she was just Micah again. No kitty. No princess dress either.

Everyone laughed, "This is weird," said her brother.

"I know!" shrieked Micah. She picked up her wand, twirled it around and she was once again a kitty.

She skipped across the yard and then back again, then she ran up the steps and back into the house, leaving her family to wonder what was going on.

Micah hurried to her room followed by her three kittens. She closed the door, put the wand on her bed and was suddenly in her pajamas again.

"Micah."

Micah spun around. "Who is that?"

In the corner of her room for just a brief second, she saw the crow, the one that had almost hit her. But then the crow was a man, with white hair and a white beard.

Micah backed away until she bumped into her closet door. She was terrified.

The man was starting to fade away, and then he was gone.

Micah realized she was holding her breath. She slowly let the air out of her lungs and sank to the floor.

She held the wand in her hands and closely inspected it.

It just looks like a plastic wand with a Hello Kitty top.

Even though she wanted to be a kitty today, she wasn't sure what to do. She knew her parents were worried, and now she had seen a bird and an old man in her room. She stared at the corner where they had been.

Maybe I'm crazy.

Micah slumped against the closet and thought for a few seconds.

"No, I'm not crazy, but I'm not sure what to do with this right now."

She turned and pulled her closet door open, found her special Hello Kitty box, lifted the lid, and carefully placed her wand inside.

She closed the box, closed her closet, and then stood and walked to the window. She pulled back the curtain to look outside. Instinctively she looked up into the sky.

She couldn't see the bird, or the old man, but somehow, she knew they were there.

Micah smiled. *Dreams really do come true.*

∽ 17 ∾

ONE TOUGH LITTLE KID

As the movie drew to a heroic end, Alex snatched his plastic sword and jumped from the sofa. Assuming the exact same position as his superhero, Alex joined in the revelry of, yet another ruthless criminal removed from the streets by Captain America.

Satisfied with the exemplary accomplishment, Alex held his position—crouched with sword in hand, until the credits began rolling and Captain America disappeared from the screen.

"Alex?"

Three-year-old Alex jumped when his dad called him from the front hall.

"Yeah, Dad?" Alex carefully placed his sword on the floor next to the television, then ran to his dad.

His parents were standing near the front door.

"Daddy's leaving for work, Alex."

Alex leaped into his dad's open arms and threw his own arms around his dad's neck.

"Be a good boy today and help mommy," said Dad, as he carried Alex out onto the front sidewalk.

Alex nodded, "I will, Daddy." His eye caught sight of the motor-cycle. "Are you riding your bike, Daddy?"

Dad stood Alex on the cement and gave Mom a kiss. "Yeah—I need to change the oil today."

"Can I ride with you?"

"Sorry, Buddy, not today, I'm running late. Maybe after work." Dad swung his leg over the bike and plopped onto the black seat.

Usually when Dad rode his motorcycle to work, he would give Alex a quick ride around the block before he left, but today he didn't have time.

The engine rumbled when Dad turned the key, and Alex watched until the shiny bike and Dad disappeared around the corner.

Alex was surprised to see an old man with long white hair standing on the sidewalk at the end of the driveway. He reached for his mom's hand to tell her, but when he turned around the man was gone.

The familiar sound of his dad's bike roared in the distance until Alex and Mom stepped inside the house and Mom closed the door.

Alex ran through the living room and kitchen and burst through the back door. "I'm playing outside, Mom!"

Mom laughed, "Okay." Was all Alex heard.

Even early this morning, the California sun beat down on Alex's plastic swimming pool. Left from yesterday's play, a few toys still floated silently in the nearly three inches of warm water.

One at a time, Alex retrieved the toys from the pool and tossed them onto the grass. He knelt and began swishing his hand through the water. Soon, blades of grass and bits of dirt surfaced from their quiet resting place on the bottom of the shallow pool.

Alex looked up when he heard a loud sound overhead.

A huge black crow was flying directly at him, and Alex covered his head with both hands. The crow came within inches of Alex's head and then darted into the sky. Alex didn't wait to see if it would return. He jumped up and ran screaming into the house.

Mom was standing at the kitchen counter and whirled around when Alex burst through the door.

"What's the matter, Alex?" Mom moved quickly around the counter and knelt next to Alex.

"There was a—a big black—a big black bird in the back yard." Alex was crying now, and Mom hugged him.

"Did it hurt you?"

"N…no. But…but it almost hit me!" wailed Alex.

Mom hugged him tight. "I'm sorry," she said softly and stroked his blonde hair.

Alex sniffled, "Will you come outside with me?"

Mom stood and took Alex's hand and they both went out into the back yard. The crow he had seen was nowhere to be found.

Alex held tightly to his mom's hand.

"You're shaking, Alex," said Mom and she picked him up.

Alex's entire body was tingling, and he rested his head on Mom's shoulder as she sank into a patio chair.

The two sat quietly, Mom humming a song and Alex peeking through his long eyelashes scanning the sky for the mischievous bird. He couldn't see any sign of it but when Mom suggested they both go inside he readily agreed.

Where is Captain America when I need him?

Alex accepted a welcome glass of juice and settled into a chair at the kitchen table to eat his cereal.

"Oh great."

Alex looked up. Mom was holding Dad's wallet and keys.

"Your dad forgot his these and his cell phone so that means he will not be able to get into the shop this morning. I can't even call him to let him know."

Immediately, Alex jumped up and grabbed the keys, cell phone and wallet from his mother. "I'll take them Mommy," and he dashed out the front door.

"Alex?"

But he did not answer his mother. He just ran out the front door, down the driveway and onto the sidewalk. To Alex, it seemed like he was flying, yet his feet still touched the ground.

He could hear his mother, "Alex! Alex! Come back here!"

But he didn't look back. He figured his mom would get his baby sister out of bed and chase after him in the car, but before he knew it, he had run several blocks and was now on the main road—he had heard his parents call it Winchester Road—a very busy street that crossed the freeway and lead onto the other side of town where his dad's motorcycle shop was located.

Alex was not sure what was happening or why he was running so fast—or why he was so brave. He had never even been off the street in front of his house without Mom or Dad with him and even though he knew his mom was probably worried, he kept running.

As he ran along the side of the road, he kept hearing cars honking and people yelling things like, "Hey little kid!" or "Where's your mom?" One guy even yelled, "Where's the fire?" But he kept running. He wanted to reach his dad before he got to the shop and found out that he had left everything he needed at home.

As Alex ran, a black bird was suddenly right in front of him. It scared him for a second, remembering the bird that almost hit him. But it didn't look at him, and it flew low, almost at Alex's eye level. It seemed kind of friendly.

Alex kept running.

But then the bird turned to look at him, only now the bird looked like an old man, like a grandpa. Then it was a bird again.

Alex kept running.

Even with Alex's three-year-old logic he knew what had happened. Dad had been in a hurry, and he was used to his wallet and cell phone sitting on the seat of his truck. When he took the bike today—he just forgot.

He had heard his dad say many times that he needed to put a house key and a shop key on the motorcycle keys, but Alex guessed Dad hadn't done that yet.

Now he was crossing a main intersection and passing a big school. He kept running straight, even though it was such a busy road. He knew this was the way dad always drove to work. As he came toward another main road the traffic was completely stopped—this was just before the hill that crossed over the freeway.

"Hey little boy!"

Alex turned around quickly—a policeman was running toward him. But Alex didn't stop. Instead, he darted among the stopped cars searching frantically for his dad's motorcycle.

Alex saw the string of streetlights turn green, but the cars didn't move and soon the lights turned yellow and then red again.

A lady opened her car door, "Hey little Captain America! Are you lost?"

Alex looked down at his clothes. He still had his Captain America costume on from this morning. He looked back at the lady, but he kept running. He was running so fast he left the lady and the policeman way behind him.

"Alex!"

Dad's familiar voice caught Alex's attention and he spun around trying to see where it came from.

"Alex what are you doing?" Dad's voice sounded almost frantic, and Alex stopped running.

Dad's worried expression startled Alex and he quickly held up the three things his dad had forgotten, hoping his dad would not be mad.

Saying nothing, Dad scooped Alex up in his arms and made his way through the menagerie of stopped cars to his motorcycle.

Alex was confused. Dad seemed to be crying.

Dad climbed onto the motorcycle and sat Alex in front of him. It was several seconds before the traffic started to move, and when it did, Dad slowly guided the bike through the cars out of the traffic and into the Taco Bell parking lot.

Alex noticed that the cars seemed to just let dad go around them. Alex had never seen the cars stop like that before.

Maybe dad's going to buy me a taco…

Dad turned the motorcycle engine off, but he didn't say anything.

Alex noticed Dad's hands were shaking when he took his cell phone from Alex's tight grip. Dad punched in some numbers and then Alex heard his mom's sobbing voice through the speaker on Dad's phone.

"He's right, here, Honey." There was a pause, but Alex could still hear mom crying.

"I have him. I don't know. He was running down the side of the road almost to the freeway." Another pause.

"Where are you? Okay, okay. We'll wait here."

Dad dropped his cell phone into his pants pocket and rubbed his eyes.

Alex wasn't sure what to do. Dad didn't seem mad, but now that Alex thought about it—he had never run away from his mom before and certainly not into traffic on busy streets.

Dad turned Alex around on the seat, so he was facing him. Suddenly Alex produced the keys and his dad's wallet.

Dad chuckled and pulled Alex into a tight hug. "Alex how did you—what made you?" Dad stopped.

Alex tried to pull away to look at his dad, but he couldn't. His face was buried in his dad's jacket, so he just sat there.

Finally, when dad released him, Alex grinned. "I—I just wanted to bring you your stuff so you could get into your shop."

Dad shook his head in bewilderment and still said nothing.

It was several minutes before Mom pulled into the parking lot. She jumped from her car leaving the door open and ran to Alex and dad, throwing her arms around them both.

Alex was now starting to think about what he had done. For some reason he didn't even think about running out the door. He had never done that before—he wasn't even allowed in the front yard alone.

His three-year-old thoughts drifted to just an hour or so ago. To the swimming pool. The little fragments of grass floating on top of the water. He suddenly saw something in his mind that he had not seen this morning.

A shadow—the shadow of the bird looming over the shallow water.

Alex's heart leaped. He had a superpower. He really, really did! He could run super-fast just like he always wanted to.

He looked at his mom and dad. He glanced at the car and could see his baby sister in her car seat playing with her feet.

He looked at his mom and dad again. They didn't seem mad. But they didn't seem happy either.

"That's one tough little kid you got there," a policeman called to mom and dad and waved before he got on his motorcycle and drove away.

"Mommy and Daddy?"

His parents were both looking at him. Both of their eyes were red, but they waited for Alex to say something.

Alex's little heart was pounding. He leaned toward them and giggled, "I can run really, really fast."

Dad looked at Mom and they both turned back to Alex and dad's lips curled into a weak smile.

"That's really cool, Alex."

He leaned into his dad's shoulder hugging him tight.

Over by the door to Taco Bell, the same old man from this morning was smiling at Alex, and then he walked around the corner and disappeared.

Alex sat back up and grinned at his dad. "I know," then he whispered, "Like Captain America."

❧ 18 ❧

LITTLE PEOPLE CAN HAVE BIG SKILLS

DAD CAME IN from the garage carrying a huge black framed mirror. "Maybe we can get this hung today. I picked up some anchor bolts."

Mom was just finishing feeding Audrey her breakfast.

Dad leaned the mirror against the cabinet. He went back to the garage and returned with a ladder

"Could you get the hammer out of the drawer and let's see if we can get this thing up today?"

"Let me put Audrey in the back yard with her brother." Mom lifted Audrey out of the highchair, scooped up a couple of toys and then pushed the partially open back door with her foot so she could go out.

"Did you forget to close the back door, Son?"

Audrey's older brother was playing on the grass, and he looked up from his trucks. "Sorry, Mommy."

"Its' okay," said Mom, "but could you keep an eye on your sister? Daddy needs my help for a few minutes."

"Uh huh," mumbled Audrey's three-year-old brother.

Mom sat Audrey in the playpen and handed her a toy with wooden beads that traveled over twisted metal tracks when Audrey pushed them. Audrey immediately began slapping at the beads.

Audrey's brother left his trucks and walked over to the playpen. He leaned over the side and started pushing the beads faster for his sister.

Aubrey giggled as she tried to catch his hands.

Mom watched them for a few seconds until Dad called, "Are you coming? I'm up on the ladder."

Mom started to go back toward the house when a shrill sound pierced the air.

The sound was so loud that Dad jumped off the ladder and ran from the house to his family.

He shielded his eyes from the sun with his hand. "What the heck…?"

But before Mom could respond, a huge black crow swooped directly toward Audrey.

Both Mom and Dad ran toward their baby daughter and Dad snatched her from the playpen just as the crow turned sharply and darted straight up into the sky.

Mom ran to her son and picked him up, "Are you okay?"

Audrey's brother looked startled, and he was looking up at the sky, "Yes, Mommy."

Dad and Mom stood quietly for a few minutes, each holding one of their two children.

"I've never seen anything like that," said Dad. He held his baby daughter away from him and quickly scanned her entire body. "She doesn't seem to have a scratch."

"I don't think it actually touched her," said Mom.

"Well, it came too close." Dad looked up in the sky again, "I can't see it any longer."

"Was that a crow? It seemed kind of big for a crow," said Mom.

"I think it was a crow, but it wasn't just big, it was huge. Freaky huge."

They both looked curiously at Audrey. Her face wore a huge grin, and she was cooing, little bubbles spilling from her pursed lips.

Dad laughed, "I don't think she even noticed the stupid bird."

"It was big and black," said Audrey's brother.

"Yes, it was," said Mom, "and I think you two should play in the house for a while till we get the mirror hung, then I will come outside with you."

Audrey's brother began protesting, but Mom was not giving in.

"That bird came very close to your sister. It could have hurt either of you. Come in for few minutes, we'll come back out, I promise."

Audrey giggled—still cooing and now pointing at the sky.

"She probably thinks it was cute," said Dad, as the family stepped into the house, and he closed the door behind them.

Dad leaned toward the window and scanned the sky once again. "Humph," he said, and then he sat Audrey on the carpet. He handed her a toy and then got some books for his son.

"Maybe you could tell Audrey a story." Dad handed his son a couple of the picture books.

"Okay, Daddy."

Mom and Dad went back to hanging the mirror and Audrey's brother flipped through the pages of a picture book making up a story as he went.

Audrey was entertained for a few minutes, but soon lost interest.

"Audrey doesn't want a story, Mom, can I go back outside?"

"We're almost finished here," said Mom. "I don't want you to go out there without me right now."

He started to grumble, but instead picked up his dump truck from the toy box. He also got two more trucks and put them on the floor near Audrey.

He tried to interest her in the trucks, but she began scooting away from her brother making little whining sounds.

Mom glanced over her shoulder, while balancing a corner of the mirror, as Dad put in the last anchor. "She wants her doll," said Mom.

But her brother sighed, "Wait, Audrey. After the story, or let's play with my trucks." He grabbed her foot so she couldn't move.

Audrey fussed even louder and persisted in trying to get across the floor to her doll.

Dad was standing on the ladder, "Please get her the doll, Son."

Her brother rolled his eyes and carefully parked his trucks in a row. He turned to his sister but started laughing.

Audrey's whining ceased—she was cooing again.

Her brother giggled, "Look at Audrey."

Mom and Dad turned around.

Audrey was laying on her stomach. With one of her hands on the floor she held her chest up, but her other hand was extended toward her little pink doll. Audrey's eyes were fixed on the doll.

Repeatedly she opened and closed her fist. She kept doing it over and over.

Audrey's dad, mom and brother were shocked at what happened next.

Her small pink doll was on the floor a few feet away from Audrey. Slowly, it lifted off the floor and moved through the air toward Audrey.

Audrey giggled as the doll came to a rest on the floor right in front of her. She grabbed the doll by the arm then rolled onto her back. She giggled even more when she buried her face in the dolls squishy body.

Her brother turned to his parents who were both standing perfectly still.

The only sound in the room was Audrey's cooing and giggling as she played with her doll.

"What was that?" Dad's voice rose two octaves.

Mom was shaking her head, "I have no idea."

Abruptly, Audrey stopped cooing and turned toward the window.

Mom and Dad turned too.

"It's the bird again!" said her brother.

Mom looked at Audrey who was looking right at the bird. She was motionless, just staring.

Dad bolted for the door, but when he went outside the bird had vanished again.

"Okay this is not funny," said Dad. "I don't know what to make of this."

He pulled his phone from his pocket and punched in some numbers.

"Who are you calling?" asked Mom.

"911, maybe this bird is dangerous. Maybe it escaped from the zoo or something."

Mom looked curiously at Audrey. She was playing with her doll again, but suddenly she stopped. She looked at her brother and then at his trucks.

Reaching with one hand, she did the same thing again. Opened and closed her fist. The big dump truck began rolling toward her.

"Dad!"

Dad turned around in time to see the toy truck rolling towards their baby daughter.

Mom's eyes were wide. She stared at her baby who seemed oblivious to the commotion she was causing.

"I'll—I'll call back," Dad was saying into his phone. He dropped his cell phone on the counter and walked slowly toward his daughter.

The truck was by Audrey now and she went back to playing with her doll.

"Dad and Mommy," said her brother, "Audrey is magic!"

Audrey cooed even louder.

❧ 19 ❧

Belize

ONE YEAR LATER

Dede's heart leaped as the island came into view. Glistening blue waters, lapping lazily against pristine white beaches and massive palm trees swaying against an azure sky, never ceased to take her breath away, no matter where it was, but this place was particularly intriguing.

She leaned closer to the small window as her son's plane banked sharply, passing over several grass-covered bungalows. They were standing in the water and Dede wondered what they were for.

Hmm? Those are new.

She sat up in her seat and leaned even closer to the window, craning her neck until she could no longer see the small village on stilts.

"Almost there Ms. Nessumsar—looks like Biorn is already here."

Dede pressed her nose against the glass, "Yes I see him, too!"

Shane's easy laugh drifted through the speakers, "What has Biorn so excited? He won't tell me anything."

Dede rested her elbows on the armrest of the leather chair and plopped her chin in her hands, "I have no idea." She smiled as she watched her son and daughter-in-law walk toward the runway.

Biorn and Aiko waited as the plane taxied to a stop and then crossed the sand to the runway. A younger man that Dede didn't

162

recognize was already pushing the steps to the plane, and when the engine shut off, Dede hurried to the door. It wasn't like she had to wait for others to disembark. She was the only passenger.

When she reached the bottom of the steps, Biorn pulled her into a hug, "Hey Mom, how was your flight?"

"Perfect as usual—Shane is always nice to fly with. I rode in the cockpit part of the way."

Shane walked past them and grinned, "Hard to mess up with a plane like that." He waved to Biorn. "I'll be on my way again in about twenty minutes."

Dede turned to Aiko, "What kind of a plane is that anyway? It's pretty fancy."

"It's a Learjet, a midsize one I think."

Dede shrugged and Aiko laughed.

"Okay, thanks Shane," Biorn grabbed his mom's bag, "is this all you brought?"

Dede looked around her. "What do I need besides a bathing suit and flip flops?"

"That's true," agreed Aiko, and she linked arms with Dede. "I'm so glad you could come."

Biorn waved to the man who had moved the steps. Dede thought he appeared to be of Indian ethnicity. As he approached, Biorn introduced him, "Mom this is Dalbir, he started work here about a month ago."

Dalbir stretched his hand toward Dede, and she clasped it. His heavy Indian accent assured Dede she had been right.

"I'm happy to meet you, Ms. Nessumsar."

Dede smiled, "Dede, please. Nice to meet you Dalbir. I hope my kids aren't working you too hard."

Dalbir laughed, "No, they take good care of me," and he gave Biorn a quick nod. "I'll get back to the plane now."

"Thanks, Dalbir," said Biorn, "Shane said he is leaving again in about twenty minutes."

Dalbir gave Biorn a half salute and grinned, his white teeth glistening against his dark skin.

"He seems like a nice man," said Dede.

"The best," said Aiko, "he has a wife and two little girls. We are hoping to move them here within the year so he can see them more often.

"Where do they live now?"

"In Belize City, but we met him when we stayed on Tabacco Caye when we were here looking for this island. Dalbir was working on that island as caretaker for the vacation cottages. He and Biorn struck up a friendship, and when we realized we could use some help here, Biorn went back to find him, hired him and here he is."

"He takes the plane to Belize City once a month to see his family, but if we bring them here, he can be caretaker of this place when we are gone and help when we're here. It's a win, win for all of us," said Biorn.

"Except for when the kids are in school, they may stay in Belize City, they haven't worked out the details yet," said Aiko.

Dede changed the subject, "Did you kids build some new huts? I saw them when we were flying in."

Biorn and Aiko both laughed. "Hardly huts, Mom," said Biorn, "but yes, they're new."

"Are you opening a resort?"

"No—the *huts* are part of the surprise," said Aiko.

The three walked across the sand to a waiting hummer.

"This is new too?" asked Dede.

"Yeah—part of the surprise."

"You bought me a hummer? Thanks! How do I get it home?"

Biorn rolled his eyes, "it's my Hummer, not yours."

"Mom, wait!"

Dede turned to the sound of her youngest daughter's voice. Dressed in shorts and a tank top, Janae ran toward them removing her earbuds as she jogged to a stop.

Janae hugged her mom, "Sorry I'm all sweaty."

Dede hugged her back, "You know I don't care about that. Are you here alone?"

"No…no, the kids are here. The older boys are div…ing," Janae glanced at her brother.

"So, the kids are here, too?" Dede couldn't contain her excitement.

Aiko glanced sideways at Janae, and Dede noticed her daughter's eyes widen.

"What?"

Aiko laughed as they piled into the hummer. "Some of them are here, they are on the other side of the island," she patted her husband's shoulder, "Biorn figured as long as he had the help, he might as well put them to work."

Dede sat in the front seat next to her son and the two girls climbed into the seat behind them. She looked over her shoulder. The inside of this vehicle seemed to go on forever.

"Pretty tough work all right. They're learning to fly," said Biorn.

"Who is teaching them that? Do you have another small plane?"

"I don't…" Biorn seemed to catch himself but then went on, "Emmett and Tatiana do, but not a plane, a helicopter."

"Since when?"

"Since just recently," said Biorn. "I think it's his new toy."

"Pretty expensive toy I would say."

"True," said Janae, "but you know Emmett—he'll get tired of it and get something else, so we decided to take advantage of it and use it for flying lessons this week."

"I'm surprised they haven't told me."

"They just got it. Maybe that's why." Biorn didn't look over at her.

Dede suddenly felt concerned. "Who is teaching them?" She loved her son-in-law to death, but she didn't think he had much experience flying a helicopter—not that no experience would stop him.

"Not Emmett, Mom, duh," Janae laughed, "I have some friends who own a helicopter and give lessons in Newport Beach, so we paid them to come here for a few days to teach some of the kids."

Dede observed the lush green vegetation and more white beaches, "Gee that must have been a painful decision for them."

She sighed and then added, "as long as none of them get killed."

"Oh, Mom, no one is going to die." Biorn assured her.

Mom nodded. "Okay, but why are they learning to fly?"

No one responded immediately, but then Janae said, "Why not?"

Of course, why not?

Seeing she wasn't going to get an answer from her son, or the girls for that matter, she turned her attention to the inside of the hummer as they drove along the shoreline. "How many does this thing seat? It's huge."

"Twelve—I know it seems kind of big for this island but there's a reason for that," said Biorn.

"All part…" Janae's eyes sparkled.

Dede looked from Janae to Aiko and then to Biorn. "You're not telling me anything are you?"

"Nope!" the three chorused.

Some of Dede's other children, Brooke and Tiago, Richard, and Amanda, and Tatiana and Emmett, were waiting at the beach house but had no intention of letting their mother know they were there until the next day.

"Do you think she suspects anything?" asked Brooke, Dede's oldest daughter. She and her husband Tiago and their three kids had arrived earlier this morning.

Dede's middle son, Richard, was peering from an upstairs bedroom window when the hummer pulled up to the house. He saw Janae climb out, "Well she knows Janae's here—looks like she met them at the plane."

"She went for a run and met them for a ride back. That was part of the plan," said Dede's middle daughter, Tatiana.

Richard's wife seemed puzzled by that comment. "Why, if we are trying to surprise her?" asked Amanda.

"I think Biorn told Mom that he invited everyone, and the ones that could come did. It wouldn't seem weird for Janae to be here, financially I mean," said Tatiana. "After all, Mom doesn't know much about our financial situations."

Suddenly Janae bolted through the bedroom door, "Mom knows some of the kids are here."

"How did she find that out?"

"Biorn kinda sorta slipped and said the kids are learning to fly…"

"She knows his kids are here, but not the rest of us, right?" asked Tiago.

"Yes, but the slip up was that Biorn told Mom the helicopter is yours, Emmett."

Emmett laughed, "I'll bet she got a laugh out of that."

"She just said she hoped no one would get killed."

That brought a chorus of hushed laughter from the entire group.

Brooke pumped the air with both hands, "Shhh, they're probably in the house."

"Just now coming in," said Richard, who had been holding vigil at the window.

In seconds, Aiko opened the bedroom door and quickly closed it behind her. "Okay—Biorn fixed the helicopter thing. She thinks the guys giving the flying lessons brought it here—not Emmett and Tatiana."

There was a mutual sigh of relief. Dede's kids had been putting this surprise together for nearly six months and they didn't want anything to get messed up.

"Like I would turn my helicopter over to someone I don't know to fly it in Belize!" said Emmett.

"She does know about your new job as Regional Manager for the store—she thinks you had to go to a convention. *And* that you were feeling particularly generous."

Emmett laughed, "Yeah, well, I'm not that generous, but okay."

"Janae already spilled the beans that her kids are here," said Aiko.

"Welllllll, it just came naturally," whined Janae.

Richard laughed, "I told you not to meet the plane. You're just way too—talkative—you can't keep a secret."

Janae smacked her big brother on the shoulder, "Yes I can—I have kept this secret for six months and I talk to Mom nearly every day. And besides, look who's calling me talkative?"

Tiago rolled his eyes, "That's pretty much a tossup, especially if you throw Tatiana into the mix." He paused when he received glares from his three in-laws and then quickly added, "you know, a tossup with all of you!"

They all laughed because they knew he was right. It seemed all of Dede's kids—and her for that matter—always had plenty to say.

"Whatever." Tatiana dismissed his comment with a flick of her hand and Tiago laughed.

Then she continued, "yeah, that part has not been easy. I can't believe how many times I've almost told her in daily conversation."

"Well, it won't be long now. I'm excited!" said Amanda.

"This is going to be pretty cool for her to find out," said Richard, "who would have guessed—our family?"

They were all silent and then Tiago quietly said, "I think it's cool, too. Think of the good that can come of it, that *has* come of it."

"Or bad?" said Emmett.

"Not bad—it's all in how we teach them, and what we allow them to do." Said Tatiana.

"I hope you're right," sighed Emmett.

Tatiana laughed. "What? You know I'm always right!"

"Yeh Emmett, what's the matter with you?" said Brooke.

"Someone has to keep her grounded," laughed Emmett.

"When are James and Alice getting here?" asked Amanda.

"Later tonight. They are in Houston now—Shane probably already left to go get them," said Aiko, then she turned to Janae, "we need to go back downstairs, Janae. Your mom will wonder where we went."

Janae followed her sister-in-law, she turned just before she closed the door, "now you kids be good."

Richard threw a pillow at her, and it landed with a thud on the closed door.

Dede was staying in one of two small cottages near the beach house. Consisting of a bedroom and bath with large sliding doors on one entire wall and a patio that overlooked the water. The cottages provided privacy for guests if they wanted it. Meals were prepared in the beach house so there was no need for a kitchen.

Dede really didn't care about privacy—she was excited to see and spend time with Biorn and Janae and their families. But the kids were on the other side of the island, so Biorn promised they would drive over right after lunch.

After getting settled, she changed into leggings and a comfortable shirt and started the short walk to the house through thick native foliage and palm trees.

Biorn and Aiko had acquired the island about five years ago but hadn't had any plans for it. Now for the past three years they had been making improvements and living here on and off, but it seemed more so the past year. Biorn had built a shallow well for most of their water, but the drinking water they brought in, and he had warned her the last time she was here, only to drink that. The large garden area boasted local vegetables, and Biorn explained besides what they had brought in themselves, their diet consisted mostly of those vegetables and fish.

Her oldest daughter immediately came to mind. *Brooke hates fish—she would literally die here.*

Dede had been here only twice before—once when they first bought the island and again after the beach house was completed, but that was all within the first year. She hadn't been here since.

Biorn's son and daughter were thirteen and ten—but when Dede had expressed concern about their schooling, Aiko had explained that they bring a tutor with them to keep the kids up to speed.

Dede sighed. Of course, why hadn't she thought of that? However, they were in California most of the year, and here in the summer, so the kids probably didn't suffer too much anyway.

She emerged from the palm trees and stepped into a small clearing before she reached the board walkway. She stopped. *What was that?*

Dede stood still for several seconds. She hadn't heard anything—it was what she felt. An old familiar feeling—that she constantly had to push away.

She shuddered, glanced around finding nothing, and then continued her walk.

The side door of the house flew open, and Janae burst thorough. "I was just coming to get you. Lunch is ready, then we are going over to watch the kids fly."

Dede laughed, "You could have texted me."

"I know," Janae draped her arm across her mother's shoulders, "isn't this place incredible, Mom? We love coming here."

"It really is pretty and so secluded from the world. Like their own personal oasis."

"Well, uh—that's pretty much what it is—that they share with us of course."

"What does it cost for you kids to come here?"

Janae shrugged, "It's nothing really, Mom. My dance business is going well. We wouldn't come if I couldn't afford it."

The two walked up the steps and through the door into the kitchen where Biorn and Aiko were eating crab salad and rolls.

"I didn't realize how hungry I was." Dede filled a plate and joined her kids. "Why do they have to go to the other side of the island to fly the helicopter?"

"It's quieter. We built over here because it's the more protected side. It's not a very big island, so it's just a short drive over there."

Dede studied her youngest daughter who was downing a glass of water, "This crab salad is delicious, Janae."

"I know, Mom, but I'm saving to eat sushi tonight."

Dede sighed. "It's a wonder you stay alive. You eat like a bi..." Dede froze.

"If that much," laughed Biorn, but when he looked at Dede he stopped, "are you okay, Mom?"

Dede quickly shook her head as if to clear her thoughts, "Yes… fine."

Janae started for the door, "Well I'm fine too. I eat all that I need. Hurry up you guys, let's get going."

Dede ate faster than she wanted to, she would rather savor the delicious food.

Biorn opened the front door of the Hummer for his mother, "You sure you're okay, Mom, you had kind of a funny look on your face back there."

Dede nodded, "Yes—just something I haven't thought about for a long time."

"Want to talk about it?"

Dede looked at her son, "No. It's not important."

"Okay," said Biorn quietly, but he didn't look convinced, and Dede noticed an odd quick glance between he and Janae.

The small island's beauty truly was impressive. Lush foliage met with the crystal blue ocean in some places, but the perimeter was mostly white sand beaches where the water softly kissed the shores. Except for dwellings, the interior was covered with hundreds of thick island plants and palm trees.

Excitement to see five of her grandkids only intensified when Biorn drove the hummer out of the trees onto the sand. When she stepped out, a helicopter was circling overhead. She lifted her hand shading her eyes from the sun and watched as it came to a soft landing a few hundred feet away from them.

Janae's two youngest and Biorn's youngest ran to meet Dede almost immediately, and their older brothers emerged from the helicopter and jogged across the sand.

Dede pulled all five of them into a warm embrace, "Group hug," she said and kissed each of their cheeks.

The kids were unusually excited as they chattered about flying the helicopter, the island, scuba diving, and on and on.

Dede could barely keep up with the conversation, so she observed, enjoying their incessant chatter. When she could, she interjected, "Why are you learning to fly?"

Almost in unison they said, "It's part of the secret."

Dede laughed, "when do I get to find out about this secret?"

The kids exchanged quick glances, hunching their shoulders and giggling.

Dede pulled a face, "Okay never mind. I'll just have to be patient." But then she turned on them and yelled, "but I'm not very patient!"

They all laughed, but that didn't gain her any headway.

"Fine," said Dede.

"It will be cool, Grandma, you'll see," said Grant.

They walked across the sand to the helicopter. Dede climbed in and was greeted by the pilot.

"Is this safe?" she said quietly, and out of earshot of the kids.

"Oh yeah, no worries, I'll make sure they are properly trained," he reached for her hand, "I'm Daverick, by the way."

Dede nodded, "I'm the kids grandma, Dede."

"I assumed. They have been so excited to see you."

"Hey, Mom," it was Biorn, "I see you've met Daverick. I was wondering if you want to go up with us for a quick tour of the island before the kids take over again."

Dede laughed, "You know I would."

Dede loved flying. She had learned to fly in small planes owned by a couple of friends, had been up in helicopters several times, but she had never flown one.

Biorn pulled the door closed and took the seat behind his mom. Dede sat in the front next to Daverick, who started the engine. Combined with the whirring blades, the sound was deafening, and Dede put on a headset.

"Can you hear me, Mom?" Biorn's voice came through the headset.

Dede gave him a thumbs up and at the same time said, "Yes, loud and clear."

She peered out the bubble windshield taking in the beauty of this island paradise. From here, she could see that the white glistening sand surrounding the entire tiny island with just a few places where palm trees met the water, just as she had expected. The one meandering road cut through the foliage, wound the entire circumference of the island. Without turning to look at her son she asked, "How big is the island?"

"Just over ten acres," Biorn pointed out the window, "there's the beach house and the cottages."

Dede nodded, then realizing she wasn't looking at him, she said into the headset, "I see them, so beautiful, Biorn. It would be so nice to get the entire family down here sometime."

"Yeah, that's a great idea. We'll work on that."

Daverick glanced back at Biorn and nodded. The copter made a wide turn and soon Dede could see the bungalows and her grandkids coming into view.

Without warning, a rush of anxiety burned in her chest, and she searched the sky. It was there, off in the distance.

She glanced at Biorn and then Daverick. They were talking about the flight plans for the day and didn't seem to notice what she could see.

Maybe they just can't see it at all.

It didn't come any closer, instead it stayed out over the ocean, circling.

Dede could not look away. When the sun caught its black feathers, they appeared to have silver threads running through them. It was beautiful to look at, but Dede did not care how beautiful it was.

It was here because of her. That, she was sure of.

～ *20* ～

TROUBLING DREAM

"MOM, ARE YOU COMING?"

Dede's head jerked up. She hadn't realized they had landed, and Biorn was standing outside the copter holding the door for her.

Dede took a deep breath and climbed out of her seat. She glanced back at Daverick, "Thank you so much."

Daverick grinned, "The kids tell me you need to learn to fly this thing."

Dede's eyes narrowed, "Oh they did huh?"

Daverick nodded.

She twisted her mouth and tilted her head, "I might take you up on that."

She took Biorn's hand and jumped to the sand. "What do you think?"

He shrugged, "Fine with me. But I'm not going up with you."

Dede scowled and hit his shoulder, but he just laughed.

Aiko and Janae had set up some beach chairs and an umbrella.

Janae's son Zion who was seven, daughter Ava nine, and Brighton, Biorn's ten-year-old daughter, ran towards them.

"It's our turn!" yelled Zion as they hurried past the adults.

"Was it fun, Grandma?" Biorn's son, thirteen-year-old Spencer handed her a cold can of coke.

She took the coke and laughed, "Thank you and yes! So fun. I think I might take lessons myself."

Grant, Janae's oldest son, plopped on the sand. "You should, but I might not go up with you."

That brought a roar of laughter from Biorn who sat in a chair next to Aiko.

Dede sat next to Janae. "What's wrong with all of you? I can do it."

Spencer and Grant exchanged a quick glance then Spencer said, "Well, you are kind of old."

Dede pulled a face at him, "Old is only in your mind. I'm still twenty-five."

Both boys laughed at that, and they all turned toward the helicopter when the engine started.

Brighton was in the pilot's seat and Ava and Zion were waving.

Dede's heart jumped watching the copter lift off with her granddaughter at the helm. She turned to Aiko, "Doesn't this scare you?"

Aiko shrugged and laughed at the same time, "No, it's all…I'm getting used to it."

In one week?

Dede was puzzled. Aiko was the most protective of the parents of her grandkids, especially with Brighton who had a history of distraction at the slightest whim.

Dede sat back in her chair and took a sip of her coke. She took comfort that Daverick was their teacher. She did feel he was safe.

To hear them talk, Spencer and Grant were practically experts. But Biorn brought their boasting back to earth with, "Hmmm, have you taken it up alone yet?"

Both boys blushed and Biorn nodded curtly, "There you go, don't get too cocky."

They both looked at Dede, who winked, "I'll bet you're almost professionals."

Her grandson's satisfied looks warmed her heart and she purposely ignored Biorn, who she knew was looking at her.

She was content in this moment, on this beautiful beach with part of her family. There was no place on earth she would rather be.

She wished that all her kids and grandkids were here.

She glanced at the sky. No sign of the crow, but that didn't mean it wasn't there.

From the corner of her eye, she noticed Biorn looking at her quizzically as she wiped away the beads of sweat that had formed on her brow.

She didn't turn to him, but she glanced up to the sky.

There in the distance, it circled, waiting.

The flying lessons over for the day, the Hummer was buzzing with the sound of kids as Biorn guided them back to the beach house.

"Why do they need to learn to fly a helicopter, anyway?" asked Dede.

"Why not?" said Aiko, and she grinned, "are you going to try it? They'll be here all week."

"The kids seemed pretty good at it," said Dede, then she smiled, "I think I might."

Grant jumped into the conversation, "Grandma we've been practicing all day. It's easy."

Spencer leaned over the seat. "It is Grandma—even though Grant almost crashed the first time."

Grant slugged his cousin, "I didn't almost crash, I just flew low to the ground."

Spencer laughed, "That's what I said, you almost crashed."

The two boys bantered back and forth while the younger cousins were telling their grandma about their turns flying the helicopter. Though not as heroic sounding as their brothers, they seemed to love the experience too.

Dede was completely consumed with their enthusiasm. It was so nice to have some of them together in a place like this where no one seemed to have a care in the world. Flanked by Brighton and

Ava, she pulled them both close while listening to the excited children exchange tales of the day—who went the highest, the longest and who had the best landing.

The Hummer rolled to a stop just as the sun seemed to drop into the ocean, and within seconds the kids started setting up for a bonfire. But Biorn gathered them all together out of earshot of their grandma. Instead, they were soon calling dibs on the showers.

"Where do they all sleep? This house doesn't have enough beds, does it?" Dede looked curiously from the open living room to the loft above. She could see three doors upstairs and all of them were closed.

"Nope, c'mon I'll show you." Biorn opened the sliding door and they stepped out onto the patio.

He motioned to the trees above them, "We built that last year."

Perched about ten feet off the ground and nestled in palms, was a massive tree house secured to the ground on stilts. Two long sets of stairs and a climbing rope provided entrance. Biorn explained it was one open room equipped with sleeping bags and cots for the grandkids.

"You thought of everything, didn't you?"

"I actually can't take credit for this. Brooke came up with it when we were showing her and Tiago pictures of this place."

"What a great idea. Do you think they will ever come here?"

"Who? Oh, Brooke and Tiago? Yeah, I'm sure they will Mom, Tiago is doing great now that he landed that painting contract with the Navy."

"That's true. I knew he was doing well—but Belize?"

"Mom, he's doing better than well."

Dede looked surprised, "Okay—I *know* they are doing better because they have been to Salt Lake to see Mack at school, as well as fly him home often."

This time Biorn grinned, "Exactly."

"Okay. So, when do I get to see the huts?"

"Bungalows," Biorn corrected her.

"Okay—whatever."

"Tomorrow, it's all part…"

"Of the surprise," finished Dede.

They both laughed.

Back in her little cottage, Dede sat up in bed and marveled at the moon's radiance on the water. The entire wall of windows made it easy to enjoy the beautiful scenery.

Suddenly, a shadow passed the window and her heart jumped as fear gripped her chest. "Was that…?"

She stared into the darkness, waiting. The moon provided enough light for her to see a shadow, but not enough to make out clearly what made the shadow.

Dede curled under the soft blanket and pulled her pillow to her chest. She didn't need to see—she knew, and she prayed that she was wrong. She closed her eyes trying to block out the vivid memory from so many years ago when, against her will, she committed to a promise she hoped she would never have to keep. But the stories her grandfather had told her came to the forefront and she could almost hear his words, *Elo's efforts to protect his children and future posterity had been thwarted.*

Why now? Why here in this island paradise far away from the mountains of Norway where her grandpa migrated from?

The sound of waves should have been soothing to Dede, but unable to escape the relentless memory, she fell into a restless sleep.

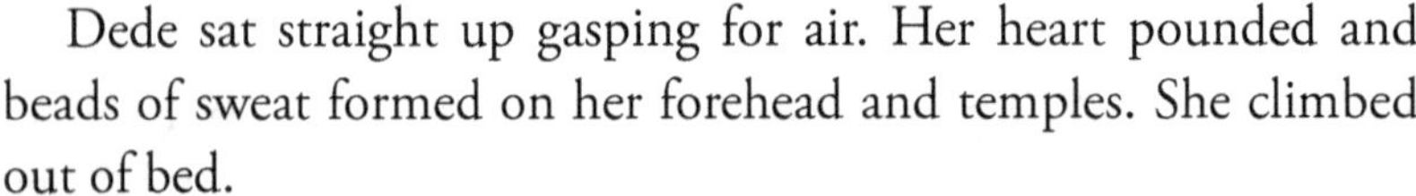

Dede sat straight up gasping for air. Her heart pounded and beads of sweat formed on her forehead and temples. She climbed out of bed.

Sometime during the night, she had gotten up and pulled the blinds on the windows blocking out the moonlight. In the darkness she searched the dresser for her water bottle, but she bumped it with her hand spilling water onto her bare feet.

That's just great. Didn't I screw the cap on tight?

She grabbed the plastic bottle hoping to salvage at least some of the water. Successful, she gulped what was left, opened the blinds, and then pushed the sliding door open. She stepped out into the warm tropical night and sank into an overstuffed chair on the patio. She wiped her brow with the back of her hand and pressed her fingers to her temples.

Why is this happening?

Dede had not been awakened by that dream in years. The story had been told over and over in her family, and upon hearing some of the tales, she had vowed that her children would never be a part of that curse. Her grandfather, Rannug, her dad, and his four siblings had to deal with it. He had managed to avoid it for Dede, her sister, and brothers, and Dede had followed suit with her own children. But her dad had warned her, she had to be careful.

Only once had she relented, and the aftermath made her swear the curse would never touch her children's lives.

It had not been easy over the years, but not one of her six children showed any pronounced signs of the curse. She confessed in her heart, that was not entirely true—she had seen glimpses, but nothing like the things she'd been told about. Her children had extraordinary talents—but she often wondered if she thought that just because they were her children. Moms are like that.

And besides, years ago she had made a bargain—and she was prepared to stick to it. Up to now, she had not been confronted with that challenge—although she thought it was happening several years ago when she was expecting her first child—but nothing became of it, and smugly, she had assumed that she, and her children, were safe.

She closed her eyes and thought of the letter she had received that cold winter day in Utah over 30 thirty years ago. Short and to the point she read its contents in her mind.

Dede Relhi Nessumasr —your children have two Viking heritages Nordic *and* Danish —you must proceed —if not —it will find you.

An involuntary shiver coursed down her spine as she recalled ripping the letter to shreds and throwing it and the envelope into the blazing fire. '*We are in America,*' she had thought, '*they can't touch us here.*'

Twenty years later her husband, of Danish heritage, had died, and she felt even more assured that she and her family had beaten the curse. Now, suddenly, she wondered. Were they more vulnerable here on this island, isolated from everyone?

She had protected her children, or had she? Her grandchildren?

Dede dragged herself back to bed brushing away the tears that burned her eyes. After what seemed like hours of tossing and turning, she fell asleep.

❧ 21 ❧

SUPERPOWERS

"Grandma!"

Dede jumped and sat up quickly, "What?!"

"Get dressed, breakfast is ready!" the words spilled from Ava and Brighton's lips.

Dede glanced at the clock, "Did I sleep in?"

It was 7 am, the same time as home for her, but an hour difference for the rest of them.

"Nope," said Brighton

Ava chimed in, "Uncle Biorn asked us to come and get you."

Dede quickly dressed, and in minutes was walking hand in hand with her two granddaughters. When they arrived in the kitchen, everyone else was already there.

"Hey, Mom, we're going over to the *huts*," Biorn laughed.

The drive to the bungalows was about the same distance as to the helicopter, only in the opposite direction. Biorn guided the Hummer and eight passengers on more of the makeshift road this time, through dense green island plants and palm trees. There wasn't a need for seatbelts—they were moving slowly, and besides, the only other vehicles on the entire island were a couple of open top jeeps so, Zion sat on her lap.

181

When Dede inquired about the jeeps, Aiko had explained her question away briefly, that they were there for the hired help.

Soon, they emerged onto a wide white beach that seemed to stretch indefinitely in both directions. The seven bungalows—much bigger now than they had appeared from the air—stood in the water before them, accessed only by a linked menagerie of boardwalks that began near a boat dock where some kayaks were secured.

"What, no yacht?" Dede chided and everyone burst into laughter.

She looked puzzled, "What's going on here?"

It was Zion who pointed and yelled above the crowd, "It's down there!" and everyone including Dede turned. Anchored in the water several yards and to their right, sat a large blue and white yacht

Dede sighed, "Okay seriously?!"

Spencer put his arm around his grandma's shoulders, "Seriously," he laughed, and Dede shook her head. This was almost too much to comprehend.

For the next hour, Dede's grandkids dragged her into each of their own Bungalows as well as the other five. There were seven total—one for each of the six families and one for Dede.

But why six, if the other kids never come here? I think Biorn and Aiko are leaning a little too heavily on the positive mind set stuff.

However, she couldn't help but be impressed—again.

Each bungalow was designed for one family with comfortable sleeping space, a quaint kitchen and bathroom, all solar powered just like the beach house. The large living area in the center of the dwellings was furnished with overstuffed couches and chairs with rattan frames. There was no table, but instead, a bar adjacent to the kitchen with six bar stools.

The grass roofs added an island effect only, as each bungalow was solidly built from treated wood to hold up against the salt air from the ocean. Windows surrounded every bungalow and heavy wood blinds on the outside dropped down and locked into place for protection from storms. Each boasted a deck expanding one full side of the bungalow with a glass-bottomed center to allow easy fish watching.

"I can't believe all of this!" Dede was overwhelmed, "when? How? What am I missing here? Have your other brothers and sisters been here to visit?"

"Uh—which question should I answer first?" asked Biorn.

Just then through the window, Dede saw the Hummer pull up on the sand. She was so enthralled with everything around her she hadn't noticed it leave, but it was Dalbir driving.

The ridiculously large vehicle came to a stop and her other four children and grandchildren piled out.

Brooke and Tiago with Dede's three oldest grandchildren, Mack, twenty-one, sixteen-year-old Harley, and Haydee, nineteen.

Tatiana and Eric and their girls, Katie, sixteen and Kitana twelve, Richard and Amanda and their five—Richard's boys, Nate sixteen, Samual thirteen, Lock nine, and Amanda's girls Noelle nine, and Micah seven. Taking up the rear Dede's youngest son James, his wife Alice and the two youngest grandkids, Alex almost four, and Audrey who was just ten months old.

Dede ran out of the bungalow and up the boardwalk. "What are we doing?" she asked, but no one answered. She was immediately swallowed up in hugs.

Even though her kids hated that she cried easily, Dede could not hold back the tears that spilled shamelessly down her cheeks. She could hardly contain her joy at seeing her entire posterity in one place. After over an hour of hugs and catching up, Biorn directed everyone to a row of chairs on the boardwalk she hadn't noticed, or maybe they were just set up minutes ago, she wasn't sure.

The adults took the chairs and the grandkids sat on the sand in front of them.

"Are we having a program?" asked Dede.

A chorus of laughter burst from the group when Brooke said, referring to Dede's years of teaching dance, "Of course, the dancing queen would think that!"

"She's kind of right," said Mack, and he motioned for the other kids to follow him. Except for Alex and Audrey, they all walked deliberately up the beach behind Mack and then disappeared into the thick tree growth.

"Where are they going?" asked Dede.

Tatiana looked like she would burst, "Just wait."

Dede said, "Speaking of wait, have you kids been here the entire time?"

She was distracted by something she saw in the sky, right above where Mack went into the trees. Tiny black dots that seemed to be circling. She tried to focus. *What are those?*

"Yeah, can you believe we were so quiet?" asked Richard.

Dede didn't respond.

"Mom?" said Richard.

Dede's head jerked back to face her son, "I'm sorry, what did you say?"

Richard looked at her quizzically, "I was just saying can you believe we were so quiet?"

Dede chuckled, "No, actually, you were amazing."

"Biorn was worried you would want to go up to the treehouse or look at the bedrooms in the beach house. That's why we rushed you away so fast after lunch yesterday." said Janae.

"The kids were in the treehouse?"

They all nodded, "Geez, I must be brain dead." Dede glanced back toward the trees, "Can you...can you kids see those black dots?" she pointed where she was looking.

"What dots, Mom?" asked Brooke.

Dede turned back to her kids who were all looking in the same direction. "No, I guess not. Never mind, I just thought...it's nothing."

Biorn eyed his mom but didn't say anything.

James's satisfied look made Dede laugh, "No we're just that good. I mean the being quiet and keeping a secret thing."

Janae blurted, "Okay, I can't stand this any longer—Mom, we have something to show you."

Dede nodded, "Okay let's see it."

"You're not going to believe this," mumbled James.

"Huh?" Dede glanced at her youngest son.

"Nothing…" Richard smacked him on the shoulder and James laughed.

Even the two youngest, Alex, sitting at Dede's feet and Audrey on her lap, seemed to be anticipating something. The excitement in her own children's eyes was unmistakable, but no one, well, except James, breathed even a hint of what was about to take place.

Then it happened.

Brighton, Lock and Zion ran so fast toward her she simply stared at them, speechless.

Suddenly, Alex jumped up, and in an instant, he was over by the trees and Brighton, Lock and Zion sat at her feet where Alex had been.

Audrey looked up at her grandma and giggled as though she knew exactly what was happening.

Dede's head was still spinning when she heard, "Grandma up here!"

She looked up shocked to see Noelle sailing across the sky right above her. She flew toward the trees and then back again landing lightly on the sand just a few yards from her.

Before she even had time to ask a question, Spencer, Katie, Kitana and Nate walked hand in hand out of the trees directly toward her, with Mack and Micah behind them.

When the group was about ten feet away, the four simply vanished and she could clearly see Mack and Micah, who almost immediately became animals; Mack a stately lion and Micah a small white house cat.

Dede stared in disbelief and fear. Anxiously, she started to stand almost dropping Audrey but just then the six children were themselves again and she plopped back down securing Audrey on her lap.

Laughing, the six ran toward her joining their three cousins on the sand. But then, Alex, running full speed—instantly crossed the space between the trees and his grandma and again sat at Dede's feet next to his cousins.

Dede was shaking now and started to stand again, but Richard's hands on her shoulders pushed her back down in her chair, "Wait, Mom."

Visions of the stories she had been told by her grandpa about his family and great grandpa, swirled madly through her thoughts. Her heart raced and she tried to force away that fateful day with her own parents.

"Grandma?"

Startled, Dede turned to her left where Samual was standing. "I see you are thinking about your Grandpa Relhi. Don't worry about him."

Dede's eyes widened. "How did you…?"

"Nor your Great Grandpa Relhi," continued Samual, and he stepped closer to her.

Nineteen-year-old Haydee knelt before her grandma and looked her directly in the eyes, "It's just the crow, Grandma, but he isn't mean."

"No! It's bad! You don't understand. You must…" wailed Dede.

Now Grant stood before Dede. Saying nothing, he simply gazed into his grandma's eyes.

Dede's fear immediately left her, and she scanned the group of faces. Everyone was so calm.

"The crow is not bad?" asked Dede but then she grabbed Grant's hands, "did you do that?" and Grant smiled.

Dede looked to her right and then to her left. Everyone but her three sons were sitting on the sand. Her boys were standing behind her.

"What is going on? When did this happen? Why didn't you tell me?" Dede began crying, "this is not a good thing!"

"Mom, it's okay," said James, "you have to trust us."

Dede pulled Audrey close to her chest and hugged her tight. The quiet baby still only grinned at her grandma.

Harley now approached from the trees. At least—*so far*—he was just walking.

He stood several yards away from the group.

He bent down and began twirling his hand above the sand—

within a few seconds a large deep hole appeared next to him.

Harley ran toward the water as the group watched. He seemed to be pulling something toward him. With a loud roar, a huge body of water left the ocean, traveled over their heads, and filled the hole, splashing on all of them. Now he focused on the center of the water, and slowly a mound of sand emerged forming a small island. Harley kept both hands in front of him, his palms down as if holding the water in place.

At that, Ava jumped up and ran toward the water. She turned around and smiled, mischievously pointed to the new island, and a palm tree appeared right in the center. She laughed and ran back to the group.

Dede's entire body shook. She was afraid for her children and grandchildren. It was obvious all of them were well acquainted with these superpowers and she had no idea how to deter them.

They do not know the danger.

James walked around in front of his mother and lifted Audrey from her lap.

Harley joined the group, as the water, island, and palm tree disappeared, leaving the glistening sand as though nothing out of the ordinary had happened.

Now Alice stood and walked in front of Dede. When she turned to face her, she was holding a small teddy bear. She held the teddy bear in front of her and smiled at Audrey.

"Bring the bear," said James quietly, and to Dede's amazement—Audrey reached one hand toward the bear and began opening and closing her fist. The bear left Alice's hand, traveled through space, and landed in Audrey's tiny arms. She hugged it to her chest and then she reached for her grandma and James placed his daughter back on Dede's lap.

Tears rolled down Dede's cheeks. She wasn't sure how to take all of this—all she could think of were the dangers that could come from it.

Her grandchildren crowded around her, and their menagerie of exclamations filled the air.

"Cool huh?"

"Isn't it great?"

"We all have superpowers!"

"Thanks, Grandma!"

Dede smiled and nodded weakly—she had no idea what to say.

"G' ma! Check this out," said Mack.

Suddenly, every child but Audrey shot high above the ground. Giggling or laughing, they again lighted on the sand and crowded around their grandma.

Dede was in a daze. She studied her grandchildren, they looked normal enough. She looked each one in the eyes then said, "So, who has what? Power I mean."

Tatiana turned to the kids, "why don't you each tell Grandma."

They were all on the sand again sitting in no particular order, and immediately they started talking at once.

Mack stood up, "I'm the oldest, I'll start."

Tiago interjected, "That's a good idea, but I think you should each *demonstrate* what you can do for Grandma," he searched the other parents faces for approval and they all nodded in agreement. He turned back to his son, "Okay to have less confusion, let's start with you, Mack, and the rest follow in age."

A feeling of excitement rushed through Dede's grandchildren and their enthusiasm made her laugh. She tried to relax, to push away the feeling of dread that had accompanied the idea of super-powers or gifts her entire adult life, or earlier. She suddenly remembered the crow and her dad on the deck when she was nine, and the look of fear on her dad's face that morning.

She and her dad had talked about it many times since, about how he had dodged the 'curse' as he called it, for his kids. And how his father had done the same for him and his siblings. But she had sensed a fear in him that day and even though he admitted he had recognized his own gift, he had never acted on it, and he encouraged her to do the same when she learned what her own gift was.

"Do you mean they are inside of us, the gifts I mean?" she had questioned, and he had told her they were inherently born in the descendants of the Relhi family from Norway, but they had to be awakened.

"Awakened?" she had questioned, "by the crow?"

The faraway look in her dad's eyes was unmistakable that day. He just nodded, patted her shoulder, then whispered, "it has to be within a foot of you. Stay out of its shadow."

So, she did. She had seen the crow many times—or at least *a* crow—and she did everything to avoid it. But twice she had not been able to escape. She shuddered as the image of her parents' car falling over a cliff flashed through her mind. The crow lingered above them just as they fell. It had tried to get to her, but she had managed to dodge it. Did the crow cause the car to fall? She had always believed that.

But Kauai was where she had to come face to face with the inevitable. It was there when she committed to the promise, the very thing she had been trying to avoid. And now, all these years later, she had been trying to stay away from anything that may cause her to keep that promise.

The knot in her stomach grew tighter and she tried to push all thoughts of the crow away.

She was startled back to reality when she heard, "Grandma!" coming from several anxious voices.

She felt a hand on her shoulder, "You okay, Mom?" It was Richard.

Dede nodded and blinked back the tears, "Yes, I'm fine," she whispered and patted his hand.

She focused on her grandchildren, "Show me what you've got!"

Mack was still standing waiting patiently for his grandma's attention which made Dede laugh. Patience was not one of his virtues.

"I'm a shape shifter," but as Mack spoke, he morphed into a huge bear. He growled, fell onto all fours, and walked towards her.

Dede automatically recoiled, as Mack morphed into himself again. He laughed and rejoined his siblings and cousins. Now it was Haydee's turn.

"Y'all need to just calm down now," she was talking to the other grandkids, "y'all are rehearsing your demonstrations and making my head spin."

Everyone laughed as she walked directly up to Dede, "Grandma, the crow did not cause the car to fall. It just fell. The crow was looking for you, not your parents."

Dede's eyes widened, "So you can...?

Haydee grinned, "I read minds. Problem is sometimes it is too much. It's best if I look right at a person I am trying to read, it kind of shuts all the other voices out."

Dede slowly shook her head, "Then I will be careful what I'm thinking when I'm around you!"

Haydee laughed and started to walk away but Dede grabbed her hand, "How did you...?" she wanted to know how Haydee knew about the car.

Haydee whispered, "We'll talk about that later."

Dede nodded and turned to Harley who was now front and center, although there were a few whispers coming from her grandchildren, and Brooke reminded them that they would have their turn.

Harley pointed to the ocean to the right of the bungalows, and everyone turned. A waterspout erupted shooting maybe fifty feet in the air. After a few minutes it stopped, and the ocean was calm again. Saying nothing, he turned to the hummer that was parked farther up on the sand, and extended his arm, his hand palm up. As he raised his arm, the hummer slowly lifted off the ground about ten feet, hovered and then gently landed back on the sand.

Now Harley turned to his grandma, "My power is..."

"Telekinesis," he and Dede said in unison, and everyone laughed.

"Exactly," said Harley, and he made his way back to his place on the sand and Katie came forward.

She stood in front of Dede for a few seconds, but then she simply vanished.

Dede could hear her giggling though and immediately Katie reappeared.

But now it wasn't only Katie, next to her were Spencer, Kitana, and Nate. They exchanged quick glances with each other and then vanished again, this time when they were visible again, they were farther away from the group and from each other.

"Wow," said Dede. She turned to their parents, "how do you deal with this one on a daily basis?"

Tatiana responded, "I have two, so at first it was frustrating because they enjoyed playing tricks on us. But now, they know that is not okay," she turned to Spencer's dad, Biorn and Nate's dad, Richard, "am I right?"

"Same," said Biorn, and Richard nodded.

The four kids trotted back to the group laughing and somehow Dede was not so sure they had been quite as obedient as their parent's described.

"Guess we're next," Brighton motioned to some of her cousins, and Lock, Zion, and Alex jumped up.

"Ready?" Brighton's eyes twinkled and the four started to walk up the beach toward the palm tree line. They broke into a jog and then in an instant they were all four at the trees, even four-year-old Alex.

Dede laughed out loud, she started to stand but before she was on her feet the four were right in front of her again.

"That's incredible," she said, "are you all the same, I mean do you run the same speed?"

"We're not exactly sure," laughed Nate, "we've had races, but we can't even outrun Alex."

"But there's a bonus," said Kitana.

"Wait," said Katie, and she whispered in her sister's ear.

"Oh, okay," said Kitana, and she grinned at her grandma.

The four clamored back to the group and Samual jumped up. He stood right in front of Dede, folded his arms, and looked right at her.

Dede chuckled and turned to Aiko, "When is lunch?"

That brought a chorus of laughter, "Are you hungry, Mom?" asked Biorn.

Dede's eyes widened, "No! I don't know why I said that?" she looked puzzled and then she said, "maybe I will fly the helicopter."

Everyone laughed harder, and Dede laughed too, but she wasn't sure why.

Samual quieted them down, "Now, Grandma," he said, "you think of something random, not to do with here."

Dede closed her eyes and thought, "Samual likes asparagus." She knew he didn't and immediately Samual said, "I hate asparagus."

Dede jumped from her chair, "You're telepathic!"

Samual grinned, "Yep."

While they were all laughing, a white kitty ran from the group.

"Who brought a cat?" asked Dede, and she bent down to pick it up, but jumped back when the cat became Micah.

"Whoa!"

Micah laughed, "I'm a Hello Kitty, kitty. Me and Mack are shape shifters."

"Mack and I," called Mack, and Micah shot him a snarky look.

Dede eyed Micah, "Do that again."

Once again Micah became a kitty, but Dede snatched her up off the ground, they were all laughing when Micah became a girl again and Dede was holding her in her arms.

Dede put seven-year-old Micah on the sand and patted her head, "Nice kitty," she said, and Micah giggled.

Dede searched the faces of her grandchildren, her eyes locking with Noelle's. "And what might you do, Noelle?"

Noelle smiled. She clasped her hands and hunched her shoulders, "I'll show you in a minute. It's Audrey's turn."

"You've seen what Audrey can do, we discovered it when she brought her doll from across the room, she can do that with most things, it seems." Said James.

Dede put both hands on her cheeks, "unbelievable!"

James nodded, "right?"

"How did you kids find out about all of this?" asked Dede to anyone who would answer.

"It's crazy," said Amanda, "but we'll tell you about all of that later." She turned to her daughter, "okay, Noelle."

Noelle nodded but said nothing. She stood but shot immediately into the air. She was so high in the sky she looked tiny, but then she soared toward them swooping just above the group before she shot into the sky again, did a little loopy loop, and then standing upright, slowly descended to the ground again.

Dede was speechless, but she barely caught her breath when every grandchild except Audrey, suddenly lifted off the ground straight up into the sky. They scooted back and forth a little in the air, but then all but Noelle came back down. She flew around a bit before joining them on the ground.

"Noelle is the only one who can actually fly," said Zion, "the rest of us can kind of zip, or something like that," he shrugged, and Dede laughed.

"Oh, is that all, just zip? You poor challenged children."

Dede laced her fingers and brought her hands to her mouth. She felt tears welling up in her eyes and she forced them back. But she wasn't upset or even overjoyed. She was confused and afraid for what all of this might mean.

"I, I don't know what to say," began Dede, and she decided not to express any concerns at this time, "I'm so proud of all of you kids. What you can do is so crazy!"

That broke the unsettled silence, and they all ran to her, each hugging her and kissing her cheeks.

Biorn said to the older kids, "Why don't you get the BBQ's going? We're going to sit here for a while and talk to Grandma."

The kids nodded and were off.

"Could we go inside?" asked Alice, "I need to put Audrey down for a nap." She looked around, "I guess Alex isn't taking a nap today."

Aiko laughed, "Will she sleep on my bed? We can all go to our bungalow; we have water and drinks in there while we're waiting for lunch."

"The kids are cooking hamburgers today," said Brooke.

Dede eyed Biorn, "I thought the diet was fish around here."

Brooke laughed, "Are you kidding me? I hate fish. We brought beef with us." She put her arm around her mother's shoulders and Tatiana and Janae quickly joined them.

"Crazy, huh, Mom?" Said Janae.

"That's the understatement," said Dede. She looked at her two other daughters and just shook her head.

"It's a lot to take in, we know." Said Brooke.

"Just a little." Dede sighed and walked with her children onto the boardwalk.

"But it's cool right? I'm a little disappointed we didn't get our *gifts*." Said Tatiana.

"Yeah, what's up with, Mom?" said Janae.

Dede scowled but said nothing. She felt a slight tinge on the side of her neck, and she turned in that direction.

The crow. Right there, on top of a post along the boardwalk. Silent, staring at Dede. She looked around quickly but no one else seemed to notice. She looked back; it was gone.

❧ 22 ❧

BIGGEST DAMN BIRD

THE ADULTS CROWDED into the living area of Biorn's bungalow. When they were all seated Dede demanded, "Will someone please explain how this happened?"

Biorn started. He told her that each of his children had experienced some sort of phenomenon—each had unexpectedly discovered they had an unusual power. He was fearful for them, that he needed to hide them, so he ordered them not to ever act on these newfound talents.

He admitted that later he got to thinking about it, wondering why this would just be his kids. He and Aiko talked about it, and each decided to call one of their siblings.

Aiko called her older sister and Biorn called Brooke. Aiko came up with nothing, but Brooke gave Biorn just a little information.

Brooke interjected at that point. "I wasn't sure what to say, so I just told Biorn that yes, the kids had told us a couple of things. Tiago and I decided to wait and see what Biorn found out from the others. Our kids are older, so it was hard to tell them not to act on the gifts, but they weren't sure what to do with them either, especially Mack, so they agreed to keep them hidden for a while."

Tiago started to laugh, "I mean, a bear? Seriously? Poor kid."

"I think it's kind of cool," said Emmett. "There are times I would like to be a bear."

Tatiana rolled her eyes, "Of course you would."

Everyone laughed and Tatiana smacked him on his shoulder.

"All of us were a little hesitant to share, but after I talked to each of them, we got together for a meeting," he turned to Dede, "everyone of your grandchildren had experienced almost the exact same thing."

"What was it?"

"A crow."

Dede bristled and took a deep breath. Her kids were all quiet.

Finally, Richard said, "Do you know anything about a crow, Mom? I mean besides the one that Haydee was talking about?"

Dede shifted in her seat. "I'm not even sure how she knew about that, I was only nineteen. None of you were even thought of, let alone *your* kids." She stared at the floor for a few minutes then stammered, "uh, no. Not since then."

Her kids eyed her suspiciously, but she didn't volunteer any more information, so Biorn went on.

"Later, maybe about a month after that meeting, I was standing in our kitchen in Irvine when I saw this bird on the patio. I was shocked. It wasn't a normal bird. It was huge. It looked like a crow, but it didn't. It was too freaking big to be a crow. I stared at it for a few minutes, then I remembered that it was a crow that came to the kids," He started to laugh and raised his eyebrows.

"I have to admit, I did not want to open that door, but finally I did, and the damn thing flew right past me into the house almost knocking me down. I turned around to see where it went and it was right behind me, but it was not a bird. It was a huge man, he looked like a dang Viking."

"He scared the crap out of me, and I tried to back out onto the patio so I could get away, but I couldn't move."

"He stared at me for a long time. He was taller than me, by about four inches," he turned to Richard, "he was even taller than you, and you're six five, right?"

Richard chuckled, "Yeah."

"He had long white hair, maybe to his shoulders and dark brown eyes. He said he was my great grandfather."

"So, from my dad's side, right?"

Biorn nodded, "Yes, Grandpa Relhi's dad. Like from forever ago. From Norway."

"After I finished freaking out, and that took a few minutes, he explained that these gifts were passed down from generation to generation until it reached your Great Grandpa, Mom. He said all of his descendants have gifts, but Grandpa and his dad, and you, chose to suppress them your entire lives."

Dede sighed and nodded but still said nothing.

"He said it frustrated him and every one of your ancestors, but you're stubborn."

They all waited for their mom to react. She glanced around the room, "I am not."

Tatiana rolled her eyes, "Oh, okay."

The rest of the family agreed.

Dede glowered at them, "That's what you guys think."

James twisted his mouth, "Mom, I think he told Biorn that *you* are stubborn, right Biorn?"

Biorn nodded, "He did. But, yeah, we already knew that."

Tiago and Emmett exchanged a quick glance, then Tiago said, "Uh, *all* of you are stubborn."

There were sarcastic comments from Dede's kids, but Biorn went on, "He said he saw an opportunity to awaken the gifts in our kids and he began searching them out, awakening, as he described it, their unique gift in each of them."

"The crow is my grandfather? That isn't possible. He seems…no! This is a dangerous thing, Biorn. You don't want this," said Dede.

Richard leaned forward, his elbows on his knees, "He came to me, too, Mom. Your grandpa explained why you felt that way— that you felt responsible for your parent's deaths—but he said it was not your fault. He said you can control some things, but not death—that is only controlled by God. You thought you should have been able to save them, but it was not possible."

"He came to all of us in the same week," said James, and when she looked at her three daughters, they all nodded.

Dede covered her face with her hands for several seconds, tears spilling through her fingers. She raised her head and studied the faces of her children and their spouses. "I just don't want them to get hurt or to be outcasts. Aren't you worried about that?"

"That *did* cross our minds," said Tiago.

"And it was a little strange having them in the house after we found out," said Alice.

"Even creepy," said Amanda.

"I actually thought it was pretty cool," laughed Emmett.

"We've all had our questions over the past year or so, Mom," said Brooke.

"Year? This has been going on for a year and no one told me?"

Her kids tried to explain all at once. The crow had come to Biorn again, right after the family Christmas party two years ago, and advised Biorn to listen, and do what he was told when he received a call from a man by the name of Tollak.

Dede sighed, "And I suppose that call came." She looked around at her grandchildren, "obviously. When? What did he tell you?"

Not until just about a year ago," said Biorn, "and he actually called James first."

Quizzically, Dede turned to her youngest son.

"He didn't call me to give me the particulars, he called to assure me that when I received a call from Biorn, that it would include my kids, even though they are way younger than their cousins."

Alice laughed, "Aubrey wasn't even born yet."

James looked at her, "Oh yeah, that's true."

Dede narrowed her eyes, "She isn't going to fly a helicopter, is she?"

James raised his brows, "Not yet. Alex has to wait till he's," he paused and looked over at Janae, "how old is Zion?"

"Seven."

"Okay, seven I guess,"

But Alice chimed in, "We'll see."

Dede could see that was the smart thing for Alice to say, she would probably lose that battle in this crowd.

Biorn picked up the conversation again. "When Tollak called, he advised me that with the kid's special gifts, they should start training soon."

"Why? Train for what?" asked Dede.

"Train for good, so they won't be trained for bad," said Richard.

"Who would want them to train for bad?"

Emmett answered that question, "Anyone who knows what these kids possess. Imagine if evil got a hold of them."

The image of her parents' car going over a cliff suddenly flashed through Dede's thoughts, but she pushed it away.

"Biorn talked to us about the island a little over a year ago," said Brooke.

Biorn added, "Tollak was the one who found it and told me it was for sale. The military offered to buy it for us, but Tollak advised us to own it ourselves. That way we have control who comes and goes."

"The military? Why the military?"

"That's a whole other conversation," said Tiago.

Each of them adding their own part of the story, they went on to tell her that when Biorn approached them about the idea for this the island—they all came together. This was a group effort and they had all been here many times.

"With what? You kids can't afford this! How in the world did all of you help? And why have you taken so long to tell me?"

"Well, you're kind of freakin' out, Mom," said James in his usual casual tone and Dede scowled at him.

"I am not freaking out."

"Yeah, you kinda are." Said Richard.

She looked around; all the kids were nodding.

Dede opened her mouth but shut it again. She looked at James who grinned. "Richard has his own trucking company now and I bought a dealership."

Dede was speechless, unusual for her.

"Mack, Haydee, Harley, Nate, and Katie, have already been on missions," said Brooke.

"And made some big bucks," said Tiago.

"What? How?"

"Some CIA agent in Salt Lake was with Mack when he first discovered his power." Emmett glanced at Tiago, "I think his name was Jesse?"

Tiago nodded.

Emmett continued, "He searched Mack out when he got home from his mission, talked to all of us and well, we have contracts with every branch of the military including the Seals, and even the Coast Guard."

"Those guys pay good money—a lot of it," laughed Tatiana.

"Do you go with them?" Dede was mortified at the thought of her grandchildren being placed in such danger.

"Yes, sometimes, but we don't do anything," said Tatiana.

Brooke laughed, "Yeah, we're supposed to supervise. I think they're safer without us."

"But—"

Tatiana leaned toward her mother. "Mom, we've been doing this for over a year. We just didn't know how or when to tell you about it."

"It's a good thing, Mom." said Richard.

"And the really cool part is that your grandfather managed to give my girls gifts as well. They don't have the bloodline and they have to work much harder to use them, but they do have them," said Amanda.

"None of them seemed to struggle," said Dede. "It all seemed so natural."

"Practice," said Biorn, "lots of practice. They worked hard to get ready for your visit."

But what's interesting," said Brooke, "they are all finding out they have more gifts. They are learning to develop their own talents, and honestly, they have more than what they showed you today."

"And financially—well, just look around you," said Alice.

Amanda nodded, "I was the last one to come into this family, I'm still in awe."

Dede smiled, "At our craziness, or…?"

Amanda laughed, "That too."

Dede nodded, "I love my crazy family."

She could not deny that what she saw today was amazing. The gifts her grandchildren had displayed, she could not begin to comprehend. Overwhelmed and a bit dazed, she studied each of the eleven faces looking back at her.

No one said anything. There was only silence for several minutes.

"So, what now?"

Biorn glanced around the room and looked back at their mom, "We go forward, hopefully with you on board."

Dede's eyes narrowed, "I can't fly," she chuckled, "well maybe in the helicopter." She took a deep breath. "We'll see."

Janae jumped to her feet. "I know we're having hamburgers, but I saw sushi! Anyone hungry?"

Mentally exhausted, Dede walked with her six kids back to her own Bungalow. The sun had set over an hour ago and the grandkids and Dede's in-laws were crowded around a bonfire on the beach. Alice had long since put Audrey to bed.

"It's really okay, Mom, and we decided the island is a great place for them to perfect their skills away from the rest of the world. People come here to train them. Daverick is from the Coastguard," said Janae.

"And the kids only use these, these powers, when they are needed," said Richard.

"Do you honestly think they will control that?"

"Well not the little ones—not yet." said Tatiana, "but they're learning."

"They're getting pretty good at choosing when it's okay to use these skills." Said Biorn.

Janae nodded in agreement, "and they have already helped a lot of people."

"Besides, they have a good mentor," said James, "their great grandfather."

They all leaned against the wall or posts of Dede's bungalow, everyone seemingly lost I their own thoughts.

Finally, Biorn said, "Mom, you seem like something has been bothering you since you arrived yesterday."

Tiago laughed, "*Really?*"

Biorn shrugged and grinned at their mom, "Yeah well besides the obvious." His face turned serious again.

Dede took a deep breath, "I…I guess I am through running, through hiding."

But she couldn't dismiss the foreboding feeling she felt when she saw the black dots in the sky. Maybe she imagined them, no one else seemed to see them. *Why can I, and why do they make me nervous?*

She shrugged. *Oh well, I guess I will figure that out at some point.*

A familiar sound above them caught Dede's attention. She didn't need to look up. She knew. Her heart quickened and she looked into each of her children's faces as every fiber of her being seemed to awaken. It was now time to keep her commitment, her promise, and Dede knew it.

She pulled her kids into a hug as a black crow circled high above their heads.

Epilogue

THE NEXT SEVEN YEARS seemed to fly by for Dede and the Nessumsar Family. The kids went to school participating in sports and academics like their friends and classmates. They were careful not to display their unusual skills in their day to day lives, but it wasn't uncommon for a few or all of them to be sent on weekends to complete *assignments* as they called them. The assignments became more and more frequent, especially for the older ones.

The family spent the summers at their private island in Belize which they named Mayajaal, meaning *Island of Magic.*

In the year 2020, an unusual pandemic spread rapidly throughout the world, and seemingly everywhere was shut down. Schools and businesses closed, forcing students and employees to remotely work from home. Countries closed their borders and even in the United States, people could not move about freely as they were used to.

Dede met with her children in early March of that year, and they decided to take their families to Mayajaal and ride out the unusual circumstances the world was facing. By the middle of April, the entire family had relocated to the island indefinitely where they celebrated Dede's sixty-ninth birthday.

The adults, which now included several of the grandchildren, decided to spend the time concentrating on skill development as even their assignments slowed down to almost nothing. They brought in skilled trainers in every area of combat.

Unexpectedly the shutdown lasted a full year, but by march of 2021 their skills are more honed than ever, so they were more than ready when the agencies began contacting them again.

Nine of Dede's grandchildren are out of school and have been participating in more long-term assignments. Mack, Haydee, Harley, Katie, Nate, Samual, and Spencer all in their twenties, Grant and Kitana both eighteen. Spencer and Grant have been recruited to specific branches of the service where they work undercover. Spencer in the Navy and Grant the Air Force, while the other seven attend college or have completed college. Their education is remote, and when not on assignment, they spend most of their downtime on Mayajaal where more bungalows were added.

The younger ones, Lock, Noelle, Brighton, Ava, Zion, Micah, Alex, and Audrey are between the ages of sixteen and seven, still in gammer school, and living at home in California, Arizona, or Utah with their parents. They visit Mayajaal often, but their parents are anxious for them to complete their education in a normal setting in the homes they are accustomed to.

Up until now, their assignments have been geared toward using their skills in under cover stings or participating in cohort missions with the military. Each one building a stronger foundation for them to draw from as the missions become more and more complex.

Near the end of 2021, a new battle ensues, and their efforts and skills are forced to a whole new level when, guided by their great grandfather, they are pitted not only against the evils of the humanity, but a new force, Imminence. They find themselves fighting for justice and sheer human survival, not only against the perils of this world, but the evil darkness of the world beyond.

NESSUMSAR FAMILY – IMMINENCE
BOOK II

"WE KNEW they would migrate here someday."

"They didn't migrate here, they were already here."

Young and anxious, Alpo rolled his eyes. "Well, someone came here first, that's *why* they were already here."

The older Viking nodded, "You are correct, but this family grew up in America—they have never lived in Norway or Denmark. It was their great grandfather who came here first." Sulo laced his fingers and sat back in his chair, deep in thought.

Alpo waited impatiently. He surveyed the others, sitting quietly, waiting for direction from Sulo. He didn't understand why there had to be so much contemplation. '*Let's just take them out!*' He had proposed earlier but was quickly stifled by other members of the council.

Finally, Sulo stood. "It is necessary to converse with my superiors. Let's not," he turned to Alpo, "to use your words, mess this up."

The rest of the council stood, and Alpo quickly followed suit. He was new here, but he did know what that motion meant.

Sulo immediately began shrinking, once a bat, he shot straight into the sky and in seconds was out of sight. The rest of the council quickly morphed and took to the sky right behind him, Alpo taking up the rear.

Erkki, one of the younger council members dropped back next to him. They didn't talk while in bat form, but he conveyed his thoughts to Alpo. *'You needn't worry. In due time there will be more action than you can handle. I promise you that.'*

Alpo shot back, *'They don't seem to want to pursue them. How can we fight them then?'*

Erkki squinted his already beady eyes, *'Because, Alpo, we have an advantage. We are already dead.'*

ABOUT THE AUTHOR

Author of *Nessumsar Family – Legend of the Crow*, Debbie Ihler Rasmussen takes readers into a world of the paranormal, adventure, superhuman powers, and mystery.

Her greatest treasures are her six children and seventeen grandchildren, who now live in three states. This project is particularly close to Debbie's heart as it was for her grandchildren that these stories were originally written.

Forty-four years of teaching dance, a lifetime of church service, random jobs, adventures, travel, and scores of treasured friends, add to her library of characters and ideas.

Nessumsar Family – Legend of the Crow is the first book in this new series where ancestors in Norway, seek to bestow superhuman powers on their posterity five generations later in America.

Currently Debbie lives in the shadows of the majestic Wasatch Mountains in Salt Lake City, Utah where she loves the spring, summer, and fall—and tolerates the winters. She gives thanks to God for her family, her friends, and the blessings of writing. She loves (and misses) the beach, running (recently walking!) cycling, hiking, reading, and fun.

www.ingramcontent.com/pod-product-compliance
Lightning Source LLC
Chambersburg PA
CBHW060315310726
48976CB00007B/2335